THROU(Ͽ

THROUGH THE THIRD EYE

THE STRANGE ADVENTURES
OF
BERENGARIA OF NAVARRE
AND
SALEM, SON OF SINBAD

STORY BY
OLCAY AKDENIZ

WORDS AND EDIT
JENNY VARDY

Matador
9 Priory Business Park,
Wistow Road, Kibworth Beauchamp,
Leicestershire. LE8 0RX
Tel: 0116 279 2299
Email: books@troubador.co.uk
Web: www.troubador.co.uk/matador
Twitter: @matadorbooks

ISBN 9781788032988

British Library Cataloguing in Publication Data.
A catalogue record for this book is available from the British Library.

Printed and bound in the UK by 4edge limited
Typeset in 11pt Minion Pro by Troubador Publishing Ltd, Leicester, UK

Matador is an imprint of Troubador Publishing Ltd

This book was written in memory of a special aunt, a wonderful story-teller, who charmed my youth and fired our young imaginations.

CONTENTS

FOREWORD

As a lad I sat for many hours with siblings, cousins and friends, enraptured by the tales of mystery and adventure woven by my aunt, a natural story teller. She revelled in our youthful, wide-eyed wonder, as her stories captured our imagination and took us on flights of fancy to places we had never been. Many of her stories were historical, others were folk-lore, but all brought the past to life for us.

As I grew older I was determined that my own family, children and grandchildren, should delight in the tales she had told, and so I set myself to write them down.

Anxious that the history should be a true reflection of the past, I have spent many years researching the authenticity of the accounts and have used the stories to form a rich tapestry and myth which I have coloured with Philosophy and stitched together with a strong thread of magic and mysticism that transcends the barriers of time and space.

I am now, at long last, prepared to pass these stories on in the hope that they will inspire in my readers the same thrill of adventures in times past and provide a challenge to their accepted philosophies, as the original recitations did me.

CHARACTERS

Berengaria, Royal Princess of Navarre
Queen Sancha of Navarre
King Sancho of Navarre
Sancho, Royal Prince of Navarre
Princess Blanche of Navarre
Lady Lorraine, companion to Berengaria
Salem el Sinbad, son of Sinbad the Sailor
Richard the Lion Heart, son of
Henry 11 and Eleanor of Aquitaine
Bathsheba, mother of Salem
Yunus, brother of Bathsheba
Masood, father of Bathsheba and Yunus
Rashid, one of Sinbad's captains
Murat, son of a merchant in Yemen
Musa, an elderly tutor
Carlos, Second Officer from Portugal
Simon alias Salem
Pierre, younger brother of King Philip of France
Signor Baggio Genovese, Counsellor to the Vatican
    Pope Urban 3rd
Guy de Lusignan, King of Jerusalem
Saladin, King of Damascus
Frederic Barbarossa, Holy Roman Emperor

Father Dominic, Padre

Philip Augustus 11, King of France

Signor Viyalli of Venice

Bishop of Genoa, appointed president by the Holy
Roman Emperor

Captain Doria and **Lady Spinola** of Genoa

Eleanor of Aquitaine and Guyenne, mother of Richard 1

Louis V11 of France, Eleanor's first husband

Henry 11, Eleanor's second husband

Prince Henry, second son of Eleanor

Prince John, later King John, fifth son of Eleanor

Princess Alice of France, betrothed to Richard

William 11, King of Sicily

Lady Louise, companion to Eleanor

Lady Sarah, companion to Alice

Leopold V, King of Austria

Queen Joan of Sicily, sister to Richard

Signor Marcos, Knights Templar

Isaac Comnenus, Governor of Tarsus, King of Cyprus

Sir Constantine, cousin to Comnenus

Suleiman Effendi, an old gentleman of Bagdad

Bella Doria, the Admiral's ship

PROLOGUE

WHEN PAST BECOMES PRESENT

The vast Universe, of which our solar system is but a tiny speck, evolves and progresses on its own timescale, due to natural forces within it, and far beyond our comprehension.

Our more immediate environment is affected by periodic cycles and climatic effects that may stretch over thousands, even millions of years.

All Nature has a built-in clock which governs its existence.

On the infinite continuum that we call Time, the Past can become the Present in the twinkling of an eye, or in the telling of a tale!

ONE

ELEANOR OF AQUITAINE
AND GUYENNE

Eleanor was a remarkable woman, distinguished in every way, living in a world dominated entirely by men. There have been others like her but at that time she had a unique influence on the tide of history. No other had been married to two kings, Louis VII of France and Henry II of England and by doing so became Queen Consort in two of the most powerful countries of the day. She then exceeded this by giving birth to three Kings of England, Henry III, Richard, the Lion Heart (Coeur de Lion), and King John.

Eleanor was born into a very privileged family. Her father was one of the wealthiest noblemen in Europe and one of the most powerful. As the oldest child she inherited all his wealth, land and titles.

She married Louis V11 to become Queen of France. The marriage was annulled on the 11th March 1152. This was a privilege occasionally granted by the Pope to favoured members of Royalty. Too close a bloodline relationship was given as the reason but all believed it was really because there had only been two daughters from the union and no son.

In two months, on May 18th, Eleanor became engaged to another cousin, Henry 11nd, Duke of Normandy, who was nine years her junior and a closer relative than Louis. They were married on the 25th October 1154. This proved a more productive union, giving the couple eight children, five males of whom three would each take his turn on the English throne, even in their mother's life-time.

Eleanor's marriage to Henry initiated the beginning of the Angevin Empire, which eventually led to the War of the Roses and the demise of Richard III. The era, which lasted for more than three centuries, was the longest in England's history.

Throughout her reign, she was held in universal respect and admiration and above all, by the Vatican. She won the approval of the Church by her involvement in the second Crusade when she led an army of fiercely fighting women, appropriately named The Amazons.

Her generous, personal contributions to the Arts and the betterment of life in general in her two countries, brought her the approbation of the people of both France and England.

(It is hard to imagine that a woman of such prominent notoriety maintained her popularity over her unusually long life. She was believed to have lived to around eighty which was very much longer than normal life-expectancy at the time. And yet history suggests that even when fate turned against her she still enjoyed the support of the people).

Henry, who had also won the popularity of the common people in his Kingdom by his introduction of

'Common Law' which paved the way to the 'Magna Carta' and beyond, claimed, as a royal prerogative, the right to take any girl in the country that took his eye. He alienated many of his noblemen by exercising this right. Following a particularly excessive carnal indiscretion, the Queen encouraged her two elder sons to try to overthrow their father. The failure of the attempt led to the incarceration of Eleanor for thirteen years. Richard found in his mother all the qualities he admired, traits, he believed to be sadly lacking in his father.

Richard's dislike for his father turned to hatred later when he learnt that during the time that his betrothed, Princess Alice, had stayed in the English Royal household, Henry, by then incapable of curbing his carnal desires, seduced the girl, leaving her pregnant.

The enraged Richard was then convinced that his father was possessed by Satan. Fearing that the evil was embedded in the bloodline and that he himself had inherited the curse, Richard vowed he would never risk passing this on to any possible offspring of his own. And so the weakness of Henry dramatically influenced the actions of his son and threatened the future of the Plantagenet dynasty.

When Richard eventually acceded to the throne, he not only released his beloved mother, but proclaimed her 'Queen Dowager', a statement of the high esteem and devotion he had always felt for her.

At that time the Dowager Queen decided that the future of the Kingdom needed her personal wisdom and experience, particularly in the business of helping her son to find a suitable Queen.

Among the numerous people her charismatic personality had inadvertently influenced there was one young woman who owed her entire future and success to the support of Eleanor. This was Berengaria, a royal princess of the Land of the Free, known as Navarre. This territory between Spain and the Duchy of Gascony, was a region of France mainly populated by the Basques. It was so called because it had never been captured by the dreaded Moors, who, at one time had ruled most of the Iberian Peninsula.

Eleanor had met the young Princess during one of Berengaria's visits to the Royal Palace in Paris and had found her pleasing and intelligent. Berengaria was not to know at the time that she had impressed the powerful Queen and that this brief encounter would later change her life for ever.

Eleanor later decided that Berengaria should be betrothed to Richard, Coeur de Lion, Plantagenet King of England, and at that time sent a delegation to negotiate for the Princess's hand in Marriage.

TWO

BERENGARIA

Berengaria was the first daughter of the King and Queen of Navarre, that country serving as a border between Leon and Castile in Spain, and the Duchy of Gascony in the land of the Franks.

Her early childhood was spent happily in the royal palace high in the mountains of the Pyrenees. There followed a long stay in the Royal Court of Paris. Here her charm and eloquence impressed the many people she met and this would influence events to come. She was fluent in both Basque and Spanish, the languages of her birth, and also in Frankish. This was not that unusual at the time and many people she encountered in her early days communicated in one or other of these languages and frequently in more than one at the same time.

Berengaria was privileged in her family being the eldest daughter of the noble Basque King, Sancho the Wise, whose ancestry boasted the famous and legendary, El Cid. Her mother was the beautiful Sancha of the House of Castile and Leon. While their marriage was initially a politically convenient arrangement, to the surprise of many of their friends, it matured into a warm and loving relationship.

The couple were delighted when their first born was a son, Sancho. A male child was so important to secure the line of succession. Berengaria followed Sancho and the family was completed with the arrival of their younger sister Blanche. Berengaria always felt lucky to have a handsome, older brother to admire and also a younger sister who would look to her for protection and companionship when their parents were occupied with the affairs of State.

King Sancho had been busy, over a number of years, building a great new palace, perched on an escarpment towering above the River Argo, the Palace of San Pedro. Due to its position it did not need the excessive defensive fortifications that scar the appearance of many such castles and palaces and afforded spectacular views of the surrounding countryside. The King, anxious to please his wife, who was a lover of flowers and herbs, had arranged to have vast quantities of the most fertile soil from the valley transported to his mountain-top castle in order to landscape a beautiful garden.

Finally the palace was finished and Sancho organised a great Tournament to celebrate his new home. Many other royal families were invited and the young princes competed enthusiastically.

Berengaria's admiration for her brother reached a new height on the day of the tournament, which also happened to be her thirteenth birthday. He had competed successfully, with bravery and skill, against the other young contestants and had earned the title, El Fuerto, The Bold.

However, when challenged by Richard Coeur de

Lion, son of Henry and Eleanor, and heir to the throne of England, Sancho could do no better than a draw.

The two gladly agreed to share the Champion of Tourney title and swore a life-long friendship. Richard chose the substantial purse and young Sancho settled happily for the golden statuette.

Later that day, at the banquet for all the guests, the young princess was given the birthday honour of being seated between the King and Queen. Before her, across a wide and very long dining table, were all the participants of the tournament. Directly opposite sat her brother and his new-found companion, Richard Coeur de Lion.

Richard was about twenty-five years old, with the healthy physique and glowing complexion of an athlete. His bright eyes and lively personality suggested one who did not waste much time on idle dreaming. At first it was not obvious that he was even aware of the young princess, but halfway through the banquet Richard stood and bowing politely to the King and Queen, then turned directly to face Berengaria. Seeing this, the entire hall fell silent. The King glanced towards the Queen and noticing her approving smile he gestured Richard to proceed.

Richard again bowed his acknowledgement and started to sing a sonnet that he had written in honour of the young princess. It was a masterly performance and was received with such a crescendo of applause that it brought tears to Berengaria's eyes as she blushed with pride and a tinge of embarrassment.

Berengaria had always secretly recalled that day with a strange feeling of excitement and unsettling, unexplained emotions.

One sunny morning, Berengaria was strolling, as she often did, through her father's lovingly nurtured garden, listening to the drone of the multitude of insects attracted by the colourful flowers. She was fascinated by the variety and was trying to recognise the different species by the vibration of their wings. She had spotted a large scarab beetle in the laborious process of rolling a ball of humus larger than itself, towards its chosen destination. She was so absorbed in her observations that it was some time before she became aware that her mother's lady-in-waiting was approaching her. Anxious not to be disturbed she continued towards her mother's herb garden. However, the servant eventually reached her and informed her that she was required in the Queen's private chambers.

Arriving back at the palace she found her mother waiting for her and greeted her warmly with a kiss on both cheeks. Curious to know why she had been summoned she waited patiently. Her mother's words took her by surprise.

"Do you recollect the young Prince Richard who joined our table on your thirteenth birthday?" her mother asked.

Careful to disguise her feelings she replied calmly, "Yes, indeed, Mother! I remember him well, he was a comrade of my brother, Sancho".

Berengaria was even more surprised when her mother continued, "His mother, Queen Eleanor, has sent an emissary to your father, asking for your hand in marriage to her son, who is now King of England. Your father has left the whole matter for me to decide. Nevertheless, I could make no decision without asking your opinion and knowing your feelings."

The response was that of a dutiful daughter and gave no indication of her true emotions. "Dearest Mother, on any important matter such as this, I would always be guided by my duty to you, my father and my country."

"That was just what I told your father, but your family would always respect your wishes."

"It is many years since we met him but I remember him as a very valiant, handsome and rather sensitive young man. I can find no reason to decline this proposal, Mother."

"Then that shall be our royal response and I shall send a messenger immediately to Queen Eleanor. I have no need to tell you how much we shall miss you when you leave for your new home. There is already a gap in our family since your sister, Blanche, left to become Duchesse of Monza, but I suppose that is usual in all families."

Berengaria was left with a mixed feeling of excitement, but also apprehension at the thought of marrying a man she hardly knew and extreme sadness at the thought of leaving her beloved family and home. She asked if she might take with her, as a lady-in-waiting, her long-time companion, the Lady Loraine.

Loraine had been sharing Berengaria's rooms since the death of her parents and the two girls had been inseparable. Sancha was happy to grant her daughter's request, as she would have been in a quandary to know how to occupy the girl after Berengaria had left, and she recognised that it might provide an unexpected opportunity for Loraine also to find a husband.

And so Berengaria left the Queen's presence happily contemplating a new page about to turn in her eventful life and content that she would have the continued company of the Lady Loraine with whom she could share this adventure.

INTERLUDE

AN ENCOUNTER ON THE HIGH SEAS

Salem and his fellow sailors cowered in alarm as a third projectile followed the path of the previous two. It was a foreign and evil sight in the cloudless blue sky above the Indian Ocean. They all feared that this one had their destiny written on it in large and gloomy letters.

Salem, a believer in the power of mind over matter, concentrated all his energy on deflecting the lethal missile but with little confidence of success. He fleetingly considered increasing the speed of their vessel in an evasive action, but the time span was too short.

In the event the ball of fire missed the boat by a hair's breadth but the vortex its passage created swept Salem off his feet and tossed him over the handrail and pitched him into the dark blue waters of the ocean. He knew by the pain in his ears and the clamping pressure on his lungs that he had been dragged to a great depth. He instinctively fought to reach the surface and as he took his first deep gasp he realised that he had, indeed, had a close brush with death.

THREE

A FIRST SEA VOYAGE

Salem was born between the two ages of supreme wisdom, the times of King Solomon and Harun El Rushed, the two revered models of logic and good judgement. This was seen to augur well for the future of the young Salem.

His parents belonged to the land of Mesopotamia, the land situated between the mighty Tigris and Euphrates Rivers, east of the Levant. Salem could not have wished for better parents. Sinbad, his father and Bathsheba his beloved mother, showered him with love and from them he learnt the value of loyal and loving relationships.

Most people can look back on an age that was special for them and marked a significant change in their lives. For Salem that age was seventeen, when his father deemed him old enough to travel with his uncle on one of Sinbad's private merchant ventures. They were to carry a cargo of cotton, silk and amber from Basra to Yemen and on to Madagascar, where it would be replaced by the shipment of sapphire and ivory which was being prepared by Salem's grandfather.

Bathsheba, as always, hated the idea of her son being away from her and she protested vigorously. Salem, anxious not to offend his mother, kept his counsel and allowed his father to plead his case. Persistent persuasion from her beloved Sinbad and also her younger brother Yunus, eventually prevailed and Salem was finally free to pursue his wanderlust.

As for Sinbad, he was confident that his son was well prepared as he had supervised the boy's education himself, and the youngster had received the best possible training from the day he left the harem.

Sinbad believed in the Stoic's principle of 'a healthy mind in a healthy body' and the boy's education had been broad, to tax both his mental and physical abilities. He had mastered the intricacies of the Arabic language and studied Geography, Mathematics, which included both Algebra and Geometry and also Astronomy. He had followed the teaching of Mohamed through the Sunni tradition, which encouraged the broadening of knowledge as quoted in the Koran, "If the learning is to be found in China, then one must proceed there."

Sinbad had observed that all creatures have a natural symmetry and only because of this could birds fly and horses gallop. He believed that symmetry or balance was the key to success in life. He could not accept that the boy was naturally right-handed and thought this an imbalance of the brain. He trained him intensively by making him exercise his left hand. He would repeatedly throw items of different weights and textures to the boy's left hand until he could catch a ripe fruit from the date palm thrown from forty steps, without damaging the fruit, and so showing the same proficiency and sensitivity that he had with his right hand.

As the lad grew, strength-building exercises were added to his programme. Agility, speed of reaction and strength were all to be important assets when he started his combat training. He quickly excelled in the use of the sword and also a shorter blade and could soon anticipate the moves of his father or teachers. Wisely, Sinbad advised his son not to boast of this ability as he may someday need to surprise an opponent with his skill.

Although this training was vital for a young man who was destined to take an important position in the world, Sinbad believed that conflict should be avoided at all cost, and he discouraged sword-play or combat as a sport, teaching that it should be used only for self-preservation and the protection of others, and even in these cases opponents should be disabled as quickly and harmlessly as possible.

In keeping with his philosophy of the importance of balance, Sinbad ensured that his son's practical training and intellectual learning were balanced by some appreciation of the Arts. Sinbad, himself, had mastered the flute and its haunting sounds had kept him company on many a long night vigil at sea. Salem had grown surrounded by this music and was familiar with the rich and complex rhythms of Arabic strains.

And so, by the age of seventeen, young Salem was an exceptionally accomplished and mature young man.

In leisure hours, when riding in the desert or sailing on the river or Persian Gulf he was able to enjoy real pleasure using the stars to navigate by night and so he could appreciate the learning he had received from his tutors.

Once Bathsheba had agreed to the journey all her previous reservations were forgotten and she set herself to ensure that the 'light of her life' would be the best provisioned traveller ever to have set sail.

She found, in an old chest, kept from her wedding, a length of fine silk. She enlisted the help of all the women in the household to stitch this silk into a short-sleeved jacket to keep Salem warm during the voyage.

As the time drew near she became increasingly excited at the prospect of showing off her son, her pride and joy, to her parents, relatives and even many friends from her childhood, whom she was sure would gather to wish the travellers 'God Speed'. She eagerly anticipated basking in their admiration and even perhaps enjoying their envy at her good fortune in having such an outstanding son.

*

Bathsheba herself had been blessed with loving parents, and was a treasured daughter. Her father was somewhat of a rarity, being an honest merchant. It was this honesty that had attracted the young Sinbad when he first met Masood, back in his travelling days. The friendship was mutual and it was not long before Sinbad was invited back to Masood's home to dine with his family. The home-life was unusually informal and the women of the family were even allowed to join the men at the table and all took their meals together. They sat on the floor of the dining area on large comfortable cushions, surrounding a delicately engraved silver tray. This master-piece was four archons (the length of an arm) wide and rested on numerous intricately ornamented legs just two hands high. Beneath it lay a beautiful richly coloured, thick pile carpet. Sinbad was surprised to find himself very much at home in these surroundings. When they were all taking tea at the end of the meal, Masood told tales of Sinbad's many voyages and experiences that were already legendary along the waterfront. While the adults merely listened politely to the well-known stories, the young ones had eyes that were bright and round with wonder.

It was after only the second visit to the home that Sinbad asked for a private word with Masood. He explained his deep respect and fondness for the family and said he very much desired to be an integral part of it. He then proceeded to ask for the hand of Masood's daughter, Bathsheba, in marriage. Masood, being an observant and caring father had rather expected this, but custom required him to show some caution and so he suggested that they both took time to consider the proposal. Sinbad should ask him again when he next visited the island.

Unfortunately it was forty long weeks before Sinbad was able to return. It had felt like a lifetime and Sinbad immediately visited Masood to inform him that he was more impatient than ever to marry his daughter.

He had arrived laden with gifts for all. During his time away, he had sailed to the Gulf of Aqaba, where he came across some traders from Byzantium from whom he acquired some delicate cotton lacework embroidery that the ladies much appreciated.

Masood was delighted to give his consent to the marriage, which took place without delay.

The wedding ceremony was a very formal occasion. Sinbad's fellow seamen, in their best attire, were joined by all the captains who were in the harbour at the time. The number that gathered was a great surprise to Sinbad for, unknown to him, word had passed along the seaways, and many of his fellow captains had diverted their schedules to be present, such was his popularity.

The male guests had a feast spread out in the garden under a jasmine trellis. This special, local jasmine formed a magnificent background for the wedding party as it maintained its glorious scented flowers and rich green foliage throughout the year. As its sharp thorns deterred predator birds it was also a safe haven for the nightingales, whose sweet song filled the night air.

Many spiced and flavoured dishes, from countries around the Indian Ocean and East Africa, were served to titillate the palates of the many guests. This delighted the sailors especially, as they had experienced some of these rare foods on their many travels and appreciated the effort that had been put into their preparation. Countless crystal sherbet carafes around the table scattered the light into a myriad colours. Bowls of fruit, flowers and herbs delighted the guests with their flavour and aroma.

Music filled the air and became louder and faster as the evening progressed. The dancing matched the music in its vibrancy and excitement.

When the ceremony finally ended everyone agreed that this had been the perfect way to mark the start of a new life for the young couple.

In fact their life together changed course that same evening when they set sail on the high tide, a calm sea, beneath a full moon and a star studded sky, as Sinbad escorted his new wife back to his home on the banks of the Tigris.

They had not even had time to unpack their many chests of belongings, including the numerous wedding gifts they had received, when a messenger arrived from the Caliph to inform Sinbad that his presence was requested at the Caliph's palace in Baghdad. Sinbad had little choice but to leave his bride and follow the emissary to the city.

On his arrival at the palace, Sinbad was escorted to the presence of the Vizier Ul as Am (Prime Minister). The vizier had a reputation for being a capable and just administrator of the State, and this was known to Sinbad, who accepted the seat next to him, out on a balcony overlooking the inner courtyard.

They exchanged the customary felicitations before the Vizier explained the reason for his urgent summoning.

The Caliphate had, for some time, been expanding its political and religious influence along the north and eastern shores of the Mediterranean Sea, as well as the Indian Ocean. That made it necessary for the State to provide extra protection for the large merchant fleet that traded with the dependant territories. Historically, the merchant pathways of the Mediterranean Sea were the domain of the Republica de Marinas of Genoa and the Venetian merchant fleets.. The Caliphate had decided not to challenge this arrangement but to negotiate an agreement with the two republics.

That left the whole area of the Indian Ocean to be

protected. As this was a new concept for the State, with no precedent to follow, they were looking for someone who had experience in this area. They deemed Sinbad's acclaimed knowledge of international waterways, particularly along the Indian Ocean, to be an excellent credential for the position of Amir el Derya (Admiral of the Seas). He would be given a free hand to organise the dockyards to produce the type of vessels most suitable. In the meantime he would have the authority to recruit and train men for the task ahead and to commandeer any craft that he believed necessary for the defence of the realm.

This was an incredible promotion for such a young man and if he had any concerns about the level of responsibility he was soon convinced by the remuneration offered. He was also given the use of the Caliph's summer residence both as the headquarters of the Admiralty and also for his own domestic use.

And so, even before they had unpacked their wedding gifts at the house near the Tigris, the young couple repacked the rest of their belongings and moved to Basra, which became their home for many years and ultimately proved the perfect environment in which the young Salem grew and matured.

FOUR

A NEW EXPERIENCE

With preparations for the voyage completed to the satisfaction of all, particularly to Bathsheba, she finally accompanied Salem to the jetty, where she hugged him tightly for a long time before reluctantly allowing him to board the dhow. She waved frantically as the boat sailed out on a calm sea, assisted by the gentle, spring breeze, until they were merely a small dot on the horizon.

They followed the east coast of the Arabic peninsula, passing the Straits of Hormuz and Oman and proceeding south to Muscat. On the seventh dawn they entered the Arabian Sea, where they moved further from the landmass to get ahead of the easterly winds. They turned again to pick up the islands of Kuria Muria on the fifteenth day of their travels before turning west towards Aden in the Yemen territories.

Initially Salem tried to earn his passage by making himself available for any work that needed to be done. However, Yunus, with whom he happened to share a corner of the crew's quarters, took Salem aside and told him he was getting in the way of the crew and making them uneasy. Yunus suggested that he should approach Captain Rashid, who was an old shipmate of Sinbad, and ask for a worthwhile assignment for the duration of the voyage. The captain, after conferring with his senior crew, decided to apprentice the young Salem to the navigator. In this position he could make use of the skills he had learnt and gain further experience. Salem was pleased to have the opportunity to put into practice some of the learning from his tutors. Consequently it kept him well employed and in good spirits for the rest of, what was to be an eventful journey to Aden.

Throughout the voyage, Salem spent his nights watching the stars and practising his astronomical studies but during the day he gazed at the ocean, mesmerised by its deep blue colour and its vastness. It was while he was staring into the water, he realised that a pod of dolphins seemed to have adopted the boat and become constant companions. It appeared to him that even the waves were in harmony with the dolphins. They swam in four groups of three in a perfectly synchronised formation.

Salem longed to be able to communicate with these elegant and intelligent creatures. He was aware that he was becoming increasingly in-tune with his natural surroundings and sought to understand more clearly his place in the universe.

Under the cloudless skies and through the heat, that would have been unbearable if not for the westerly winds which they encountered on the twelfth day, they made slow but steady progress towards their destination.

However, the winds forced them to tack out to sea and then back to shore, without losing sight of land. They were sailing in well-charted waters but Rashid's familiarity with various landmarks was also an advantage. His plan proved well-founded as they arrived at their destination in fine fettle.

Their excitement at reaching Aden did not last long after docking. The dry heat that followed the morning's chill, intensified the harbour smells, which were difficult for both Salem and Yunus to tolerate. They both readily accepted Rashid's invitation to accompany him to the merchants' district. It was situated in the walled city and occupied the north section of the caravanserai, which was about three hundred feet in all four directions, forty-five feet high and built entirely of yellow sandstone. On entering through the high gateway the group had to step aside to allow a caravan of camels, still carrying their riders, to pass into the vast courtyard. On coming to a halt the camels slowly knelt to allow their riders to dismount.

The courtyard was paved with stone slabs in a geometric pattern, tightly packed with clay to form a waterproof layer. The surface sloped gently into a channel which allowed animal effluent to drain into an underground silo.

On announcing their arrival they were escorted to a spacious upper room that was comfortably furnished for the meeting of the merchants. The smooth stone floor was covered with deep-pile carpets decorated with floral patterns in delicate colours. The walls were hung with smaller but more intricately worked prayer rugs. This all lent the room a relaxed and welcoming ambiance. Salem's initial concern at being enclosed in a confined space in such high temperatures was soon dispelled by the presence of the breeze that greeted them on their arrival and prevailed throughout their stay. He was further comforted by the fact that despite the large windows which allowed in the cooling breeze, he could not detect any of the expected unpleasant odours from the numerous camels in the courtyard below.

When the initial introductions and pleasantries were complete, Salem and his young uncle relaxed on cushions opposite the window. From there they could observe and listen, without getting involved in the conversations, as was expected from a youngster in the presence of his elders. From where he sat he could watch the many travellers, who would enjoy the open air at night, securing to a parapet wall the canvasses and kilims that would provide shade for their bedrolls. As the scene outside settled, his interest was drawn back into the room. He gazed around and became aware of the elderly gentleman who had been introduced as the tutor to the young son of the merchant. The tutor, too, was taking no part in the discussions but was listening intently and watching the procedures keenly.

To Salem's surprise, the conversation was very friendly. He had expected all business transactions to be heated and excitable affairs, similar to those he had witnessed when he had accompanied household staff to the market place in Basra. The topics were wide ranging and it was clear that the merchants used these meetings to share knowledge picked up by the travellers. The merchants were pleased to hear from the traders of the very friendly cooperation that they enjoyed with the Mogul rulers of north India, when they were within the boundary of their territories and also of the reasonable taxation policies of these States.

The seamen and traders also shared the notorious

story of the burning of the fleet at Jabil el Tarik (Gibraltar Straits) by Tariq Ben Nasser. Rashid, whose whole life had been aboard ship, for as long as he could remember, vowed there could never be justification for burning a seaworthy craft. Various arguments were propounded, but it was generally accepted that motivating a large number of men for a conquest was, indeed taxing. The men were aware that they risked their lives for only possible gain and to prevent them from deserting might challenge even the best-trained and most disciplined forces. However, while the sailors felt it might be justified to destroy an army's means of retreat, they could never accept the burning of many valuable ships.

As these talks continued Salem watched the old tutor. Although he was taking no part in the proceedings, he seemed to be a part of it in a way Salem could not explain. No-one except for Salem, himself, seemed to be aware of the old man's presence.

As the discussions concluded, their host extended to everyone present, an invitation to join him for dinner at his residence, at sundown, after the evening prayers. The guests, exchanged the customary farewells, and parted, with the promise to be at the residence in good time.

Making their way back to the ship, Salem realised that to find one's way through the narrow streets of a walled city needed the inner sense of a navigator as there were very few distinguishing features and all the alleyways looked the same. Rashid explained that all walled cities were planned in such a way, partly due to lack of space within the walls, but also because the tightly packed buildings provided perpetual shade at street level. They passed through the market place which reflected the everyday needs of the thriving community, whose harbour was the servicing facility for trade to the south and west of the Arabian Peninsula. Exceptionally skilled artisans made best use of the, not so plentiful, raw materials that found their way to the city of Aden, often at the end of long and arduous journeys by desert or sea. Although Salem took a liking to many of the things he saw, he was reluctant to clutter his very restricted living space on board by reckless purchases. This did not prevent him from lingering over a simple and thickly lined cape that seemed perfect to protect him against the discomfort of chilly dawns when he was on night watch. The jacket provided by his mother, while warm, was far too decorative for his life aboard ship and made him feel uncomfortably overdressed. He wore it only when no-one else was around to see it. By the time they returned in the evening on their way to their dinner engagement, Salem had convinced himself that the purchase of the cape was justifiable and decided to indulge himself. This would be his very first personal purchase so he considered asking Captain Rashid for his advice. The cape was still there and when Rashid saw it he suggested that Salem allow him to negotiate a good price. As Salem had no experience in bartering he decided that this may be a good way to learn a useful lesson. He was disturbed at first to see that the Captain inspected many wares, seemingly ignoring the one he was meant to purchase. He thought perhaps the Captain had misunderstood him but he had promised not to interfere, so he wandered off to look at the display in the next shop. He nudged Yunus to join him but he continued to listen to the conversation between the Captain and the trader. Many witticisms were made and derisory laughter followed the prices asked for various goods. The cape was only mentioned as a garment fit for a camel to sleep on and no price was inquired. The Captain then apologised to the trader for taking up his valuable time and in compensation offered to relieve the trader of the ugly garment for a small amount of money. He said he had a father-in-law who was as ugly as a camel and would always pester him for a present when he returned home. He told the trader he had never found anything suitably dreadful to 'reward' the old man for allowing him to marry his miserable daughter. He offered the trader one denim which he thought was a good price.

Words and gestures of disbelief followed with the trader declaring that he was being robbed by someone who had never heard the word 'integrity' and who was totally unsympathetic to the needs of his many children, at his home with empty bellies. Twenty denims were demanded as a minimum and fair price. Rashid replied that the trader's children may well be numerous enough to require twenty denims to feed but his father-in-law was not worth more than two. And so doing he bid the trader farewell explaining that he was already late for an important business meeting. At this Salem and Yunus joined their Captain, with Salem feeling disappointed, as if he had lost something although, in reality, he had never possessed it. However, the trader, sharper than they had expected, called after them and agreed to accept five denims for the garment, if the young man paid for it out of his own pocket. Salem could not hide his surprise and looked to Rashid, who nodded his approval, where-upon

Salem ran back to pay for the garment and took it without even waiting to try it on.

They found the merchant's house situated on a street wide enough for a camel to stroll down the middle without damaging its load on the side walls. Because of this the windows of the houses were high enough to prevent the prying eyes of the camel's rider.

They knocked on the solid cedar-wood door set into the stone wall. A servant led them into a large marble-floored entrance hall, where their host welcomed them. A marble fountain played in the centre of the hallway and many-coloured calling birds flew freely about the place, unchallenged by the saluki, that rose to attention on the entry of the newcomers. Following the normal greetings they were invited to join the rest of the company, who were already gathered on the roof garden. This was a spacious area protected from spying neighbours by a high wall.

The party was the same that had met in the morning, except for the presence of the merchant's young son Murat. He was a slight, pale young man about two years younger than Salem and more finely dressed than the rest of the group. As the evening progressed, Salem found himself in conversation with Murat and his tutor Musa. He related the evening events at the marketplace and Musa smiled knowingly at the trader's awareness all along that the cape was for Salem, despite Rashid's attempted subterfuge. Salem also described his position aboard ship as the apprentice navigator. He explained his role and responsibilities in detail and found Murat most interested in learning about new things. Murat had a way of turning to his teacher for guidance and support and would open his arms and lift them towards his shoulders as if in supplication. Musa responded by opening his hands without raising his elbows and then, with a nod of his head he indicated that the three young men should follow him to a more secluded part of the roof garden. They stood in the shade of a tall jasmine which formed an arched arbour and Musa, then drew their attention to the stars and the patterns that they made. Using these stars as an example, Musa explained that there was a relationship between all things in existence and that the strength of this relationship was relative to the sensitivity of the instruments which measure it. Many factors, like distance may affect this relationship but the one factor that cannot be contested is the fluidity present in nature. By its very concept, nature is evolving and changing. Musa then told them that there are certain people who are so sensitive to the emotions and spirits of others that they can read their innermost thoughts. It is important to be aware of this in order to protect one-self against such spiritual intrusions. While Murat was familiar with his tutor's philosophy and was anxious to demonstrate his understanding of it, Salem and Yunus were completely taken aback. However, Murat confided in them that their reservations were perfectly understandable and that he had been very sceptical at first until Musa had demonstrated his skills several times. He proceeded to explain that he had learnt that first he had to become more receptive, analytical and sensitive to his own feelings and his immediate environment and only then could he attempt to extend his mental powers beyond himself, to understand or control the actions or emotions of others. As there still seemed to be some confusion, he shared with them a simple example. You may walk down a busy street and happen to notice someone in the distance and as you are concentrating on them they, for no apparent reason, without any form of communication, turn and look back at you. This suggests the probability that there is a binding force between people, a sympathetic bond that defies instant interpretation. Salem and Yunus were speechless and, though still not convinced, were anxious to learn more of the subject. So Salem asked Murat if it might be possible for them to join his lessons on the next day providing their Captain gave permission. When this was readily agreed, they re-joined the rest of the gathering as the meal was about to be served.

With the lesson still teasing his mind, Salem found himself concentrating throughout the evening on trying to perceive the next move of each of the guests. He ended up in failure and frustration and decided he must just wait for the next day's lesson, in the hope that the captain would give his permission.

On their return walk to the ship, the late night temperature was surprisingly low and Salem was pleased to wrap himself in the warm cape that he had purchased earlier.

That night sleep came late and was disturbed by a strange, vivid dream of colossal, black-plumed birds, approaching in flight over the mountains to the north. The birds were carrying riders dressed in black leather boots and pants, red leather tunics and blood-coloured helmets. Their bows and arrows were at the ready and they were closing in on Aden. The birds and riders circled as they descended towards the harbour. The leading rider was pointing a long spear directly at Salem and they were all shouting at him to get up and prepare himself to fight them. Scared and disoriented, he felt himself gradually elevating from his comfortable hammock into unsupported air, where he confronted the enemy commander, who shouted at him to go back and arm himself with a weapon. In shock, he realised that he was suspended and had no idea how to descend.

However, he was shaken to consciousness by Yunus tugging at his sleeve in an attempt to wake him, as it was time to prepare for morning prayers. Still disconcerted by the effects of the dream, he jumped from his hammock and made his way to the prayer room. The Captain, as usual, led the prayers at sunrise and everyone attended, as even the harbour watch was not important enough for the crew to be excused from their religious ritual. During the prayers, pangs of hunger disturbed Salem's concentration and he realised that, strangely, early morning hunger often followed a large evening meal. His pangs were further inflamed by the drifting aroma of the delicious, freshly prepared flatbread covered with sesame and caraway seeds that awaited them. He knew that this would be accompanied by goats' cheese and milk and a helping of fresh dates that were much welcomed.

It was during breakfast that he mentioned to the Captain that he and Yunus had been invited back to the merchant's house to take part in a tutorial session with young Murat. To Salem's great relief, Rashid agreed, on the condition that they both helped scrub the decks before they left. (This was a daily chore for the sailors. The deck timbers needed to be kept moist to prevent the continually high temperatures drying and shrinking the timberwork of the ship, which would render the ship unseaworthy). Usually this was a job to be avoided at all cost but on this occasion the two young men were happy to comply.

Their task completed, they re-traced their route of the previous day, through the market place, where they called greetings to the trader, who waved a friendly response. Arriving at the merchant's house, they were escorted directly to the roof-garden where Musa and Murat were awaiting them. The two were admiring a bed of delightful, delicately coloured aromatic violets. When Salem mentioned to Musa that he had no recollection of the flowers from the previous night, Musa smiled and congratulated Salem on his memory, saying enigmatically that nature was responsible with a helping hand from Murat. Murat stood by looking very pleased with himself and sporting an air of deep satisfaction. They sat in a shaded part of the garden out of the scorching heat and gratefully accepted a flask of cool ayran, the traditional drink of thinned yogurt, served with a good measure of salt and a sprinkle of finely ground mint leaves.

And so the lesson began:

"The essence of success in anything is relative awareness and the most important is awareness of self. This means a total consciousness and control of every part of our body, every limb, organ, even every cell. Through our sense organs we can relate and react to our environment. Even the rate we breathe, or the rate at which our heart beats is affected by our thoughts and is a response to our surroundings. In order to take control of our lives and maximize our powers, it is necessary for us to harmonise and synchronise our responses to the world around us. Once an individual has truly mastered control over himself, then it is possible to extend the range of awareness to others. However, self-awareness is still pivotal to success and if personal, physical, or psychological harmony is lost, that will effectively diminish the ability to contact, control and manipulate the minds of others.

As self-awareness is perfected, other factors previously unnoticed may become high-lighted and these in turn may re-direct the character and the powers of perception and judgement.

The human tendency towards compulsion should always be guarded against as it is never based on logic which should be paramount in all our decisions."

The tutor ended the session with the following words:

"I shall give you no more instructions on this matter, for our paths may not cross again in the foreseeable future, except to say, that the fabric of nature is never as solid or as finite as it appears to you at present. Once you accept this, you may discover a realm which is beyond the normal human concept of time and space and so beyond your comprehension. At such a time I wish you to remember that you are in possession of powers that can be used for the benefit or the detriment of others. You may be able to manipulate or control others but always remember that these are gifts from the creator of us all and should always be used for good, with humility and without conceit.

May Allah and Nature be with you in all your journeys and along the chosen paths of your lives. Keep this knowledge guarded as it cannot be trusted indiscriminately to others who may, for their own reasons use it against you, against the will of Allah, or to the detriment of nature itself."

*

Next morning, to take advantage of the early tide and the off-shore breeze, the double-masted ship upped anchor and slipped into the warm currents of the Red Sea. These flowed south, to be replaced by the deeper colder currents from the Indian Ocean. The Red Sea, almost enclosed as it was by two hot landmasses, was protected by this influx of cooler water, from the evaporation that might have turned it into another Dead Sea.

As on previous journeys, they left the Gulf of Aden and plotted an eastern passage towards the Arabian Sea. Soon they turned to the right to pass the Abdu al Kurri Islands, keeping Somalia to their right as a reference point. With the southerly currents and the airflow, due to the large landmasses nearby, their progress was effortless. For Salem there were few duties and he even found time to practise his flute. To his own amusement he found himself describing the nature around him in his music. The tension of the sail created by the wind, the lapping of the waves against the ship, and the ever-present calls of the sea gulls were all there in his melodies. His ship mates enjoyed the entertainment and encouraged him to play, so that more and more he created his own airs, which he had never done before.

It was five days before they left the coastal waters and charted due south towards their next provisioning port of Mogadishu. It was estimated as another four days sailing in such favourable conditions. They were then to proceed to Mombasa, their next trading berth, where they would pick up a cargo of elephant tusks, the purchase of which had been organised by Masood in Aden. Salem's grandfather wished to examine the quality of the ivory before sending it on to a customer in the Far East. The customer had previously seen some excellent examples in Masood's warehouse and had decided that the ivory had good trading potential with the craftsmen of his country.

Salem was on early watch and behind his left shoulder the sun was about to rise. It had not yet cleared the horizon, but the light was good and the visibility uninterrupted.

The sea was very calm.

He was deep in contemplation, thinking again of the teachings of Musa and marvelling at the perfection of nature, when he again observed the dolphins. This time there were about twelve of them in the distance. In groups of three they leapt clear of the water and completed a perfect arch before submerging themselves in the deep blue waters of the ocean. Below the ship, the shallow angle of the light from the rising sun was unable to penetrate the surface and the water appeared like a mirror, beneath which was unfathomable blackness. The dolphins sped towards the ship. Three, that had recently dived, were slow to reappear and broke the surface well to the aft of the hull before speeding to catch up the rest. They almost seemed to be challenging the ship for a race. Now, still wrapped in his thoughts his vision shifted and he scanned the northern horizon. The sounds of the ocean around him gradually crystallised and he heard clearly his mother's voice as she discussed with Sinbad their son's well-being. The clarity of their voices over the muted hum of the ones around him shocked Salem. Without thinking he responded,

"I am in good health mother, and much enriched by my experiences. But I miss you both very much."

Back home in Basra, Bathsheba screamed her son's name. Sinbad jumped out of bed and ran to the window in an effort to find the source of his son's voice and how it could have carried to their bedroom. It was as though he had been there with them, and yet, at that very moment the mystic link between them was lost.

Salem decided to keep this strange experience to himself as he knew he could expect no understanding from his shipmates. He originally thought he might share it with Yunus, but then decided he would wait until he had had an opportunity to do some experiments and understand it better himself.

Although he had always found it difficult to sleep in his confined quarters during the heat of the day, Salem volunteered for the unpopular night-watch, for the duration of the journey. To the delight of the crew, and the surprise of Yunus, after consulting with his senior seamen, Captain Rashid acceded to his request. His uncle demanded an explanation for this strange action, but was pacified when Salem promised him an explanation later.

The next morning when the dolphins appeared, almost as if they had been beckoned, Salem thought again of the earlier sighting when he had considered how wonderful it would be to communicate with these graceful and intelligent animals. He considered the possibility of using the dolphins to experiment with his thought patterns. He wished them a good day with their hunting and journeying. To his amazement they responded in chorus, *"We do not understand the meaning of hunting or journeying, we have no particular destination and are simply doing the things that we always do at this time of day. But we welcome your communicating with us, for you are the first surface breather ever to do so and it has made us very happy. We all bid you a very happy hunting day and a good journey."*

Salem, astonished by the ease of communication, continued by explaining they also were not hunting but trading and told them the direction in which they were heading. At that moment, the dolphin, who happened to be the leader of the pod, informed him that someone of his own kind was trying to contact him.

As the dolphins swam away, he heard his mother say, *"Salem, I am your mother, Bathsheba, and your father is here next to me. We pray that Allah, the Merciful, will grant us the pleasure of hearing your dear voice through the air again."*

As his vision blurred with tears Salem could see his parents, holding hands and sitting on their bed in the familiar bedroom in the Admiralty in Basra. He was touched by the efforts his parents had made in order to contact him in that way, as all their Islamic culture and teaching had directed them against that which is unexplainable. They had obviously put all that aside and were now receptive to this psychic communication. Confident of their participation he told them that he was in good health, as was Yunus and the whole ship's company. They then agreed that they would communicate with each other every day at the same time.

He gradually returned to present consciousness and was aware of the dolphins in the distance warning him of an approaching storm. Although there was still no sign of an impending storm when Salem passed on this warning to Rashid, the captain did not completely reject his warning but put it aside and, as Salem had just completed his night watch, told the lad to go below and get himself a hearty breakfast. Salem, however, knew of the problems of a full stomach in heavy seas, and decided to settle for a light breakfast and some sleep, while it was still possible.

It was soon after mid-day when Salem was first made aware of a drastic change in the weather by the violent swinging of his hammock and the clatter of untethered objects as they flew around the crew's quarters and also on the deck above him. The cloudless sky had given no indication of the turbulence to come. The strong wind and the heavy swell hit the ship simultaneously and the well-trained crew, without waiting for instructions, acted instinctively. Everything above and below deck was tied down securely and the sails were shortened. Rashid called Salem close to him, to be heard over the fury of the storm, and thanked him for his timely warning, adding that good sailors never ignore such a warning however unlikely it might be. Salem, already rested was then sent to help with the steering, as best he could against the wind and waves. Three days followed of the worst weather any of them could imagine. Yunus, as surprised as the other sailors, at the suddenness of the storm, demanded to know how Salem had managed so accurate a forecast, when there had been no signs. Salem, again, avoided a direct answer and suggested that it might have been through a hereditary gift from his father, he hoped that Sinbad's reputation as a famous sailor would make that explanation acceptable. In spite of this Yunus remained unconvinced, so Salem decided that perhaps this may well be an appropriate time to share his recent experiences with his uncle and ask for his support. He described his initial communications with his parents and with the dolphins and justified his hesitation in telling Yunus by explaining his own difficulty in understanding the phenomena. Yunus laughingly, said the fellow crewmen must have thought it peculiar seeing Salem talking to the dolphins. It was only then that Salem realised that all the communications had been carried out in perfect silence, without a word being uttered. To his recollection it had all been carried out in his imagination and yet he had never doubted its reality. When he told his uncle this, they decided that they should both be present at the next attempted contact. This would both help to protect Salem from the curiosity of on-lookers and also verify the truth of his tale.

Some days later, Salem and Yunus were chatting together, when Salem noticed a bird he didn't recognise flying high above. Yunus followed his nephew's gaze towards the horizon and watched without comment. He saw Salem's blue eyes becoming almost transparent, as in a sightless person. The hairs on his hands, which were tightly gripping the wooden handrail, were standing on end as if combed. Yunus looked around, concerned about being observed by others, but relaxed when he saw, other than the steersman, only one crewman on the mainmast and one on the foredeck, all completely occupied by their duties. When Salem returned to his normal state, he told

Yunus that the bird had informed him of two strange black ships, not seen before on those waters and manned by people in unusual attire. The bird had also witnessed discord and violence among the crew. Fearing that no-one would believe them the two kept this information to themselves, but Salem did tell the man on watch duty to look out for vessels approaching from the south east. In his capacity as apprentice navigator, he asked that both he and the Captain be informed as soon as there was a sighting.

It was not long before the alarm was raised. Everyone was issued with weapons from the armoury, swords and long-bows for those skilled in their use and buckets of seawater for others in readiness to quench possible fires. All were ordered to their action positions, as there was no mistaking the intentions of the approaching vessels. These appeared larger and taller ships, but cumbersome in comparison with theirs and so their own ability to change direction rapidly could be an important asset. The master navigator joined Salem at the wheel, so that together they could respond instantly to the Captain's orders. Rashid directed them to steer out into the vastness of the ocean where they might remain undetected. This seemed a wise tactic as their ship was so much lighter and faster than the unwieldy opposition and they quickly put a good distance between themselves and the enemy. Everyone sighed with relief, when by mid-day they had lost sight of the two black vessels. Unfortunately the favourable wind that had helped carry them away from their pursuers had, to their horror, brought them into contact with a fleet of four similar vessels, which they had not previously noticed. The higher crows-nest on the taller ships had allowed their look-out to spot Rashid's ship at a greater distance and had enabled the rest of the fleet to fan out to prevent Rashid's escape.

The Captain ordered 'hard astern' and attempted to speed back towards shore, believing that the larger ships would not risk pursuing them into the shallower coastal water. He was hoping to lose the chasing vessels in the fading daylight. They had not completed the manoeuvre, when they heard a muffled thud, flowed by a mighty splash and saw a plume of water reaching high into the air, accompanied by the hissing sound of steam. This was followed, within minutes, by another report from a different direction, which landed much closer to their ship. Salem and his fellow sailors cowered in alarm as a third projectile followed the path of the previous two. It was a foreign and evil sight in the cloudless blue sky above the Indian Ocean. They all feared that this one had their destiny written on it in large and gloomy letters.

Salem concentrated all his new-found abilities on deflecting the lethal missile, but with little confidence of success. He fleetingly considered increasing the speed of their vessel in an evasive action but the time was too short.

In the event the ball of fire missed the boat by a hair's breadth, but the vortex its passage created swept Salem off his feet and tossed him over the handrail, pitching him into the dark blue waters of the ocean. He knew by the pain in his ears and the clamping pressure on his lungs that he had been dragged to a great depth. He had never before feared for his life, but he remembered it said that when one approached death, one's whole life flashed before the eyes, and at that moment, he knew it to be true. However, he instinctively fought to conserve the small amount of oxygen left in his lungs, while he struggled to remove his cape, sandals and finally his turban, as he worked to increase his buoyancy. He twisted his body until he was conscious of light above him. He flung both arms upwards with as much strength as he could muster and then forced them down to his sides, streamlining his whole body and kicked furiously for the surface. As he took his first deep gasp of sweet fresh air, he realised that he had, indeed, had a close brush with death.

FIVE

SURVIVAL

Treading water, as he gradually regained his strength, he looked around taking stock of his position. It was then that he realised one, black-hulled vessel was approaching relentlessly. As no other craft were in sight, he could only believe that the others had given chase to his own ship.

Unable to dwell on the prospect of his inevitable fate, he allowed his mind to wander and found himself again strangely contemplating the concept of time. He saw time, detached from the means of practical measurement, as an abstract dimension and contemplated the possibility of being able to fold it like a navigational chart and perhaps being able to move forwards or backwards along a time-line, like turning the pages of a book. He was jolted back to reality by the dark shadow of the ship, which had reached him and he could see a rope ladder thrown in his direction. He grabbed at the chance of life offered to him, even though it may mean a life in captivity. However, he sensed that the purpose of his captors was more discovery than piracy and his apprehension was further allayed when helping hands reached down and hauled him to the safety of the deck. In spite of this small gesture of support, once on board, he was not allowed to seek shade, but was made to stand for some time in the full sun, while the salt dried crusty in his clothes and on his skin. Meanwhile he was afforded the opportunity to observe his captors. By again employing his extraordinary gifts, he found he could read the thoughts of the people around him, and so was aware of their pride in the ease of his capture.

He was also beginning to understand their language and communication, but he wisely realised that this knowledge was to his advantage and best hidden. He felt confident that he would be able to secure his own safety and, as they journeyed south, would eventually be able to make contact with his grandfather.

As time passed, he felt less afraid and began to prepare himself for his inevitable interrogation. He had spotted a tall, bearded man watching him closely and guessed that this would be his inquisitor. He was dressed in a heavy woollen cloak of very dark brown, which extended down to his sandaled feet. His head was hidden by a loose integral hood. The cloak was held by a white rope tied loosely and supporting a heavily ornate golden cross.

Salem was eventually offered a bowl of water and some food and was allowed to sit down, but was not spared close and suspicious scrutiny.

Nothing was discussed that day, but at noon the next day a newcomer appeared on deck and it was obvious from his dress that he held a position of high rank in the fleet. The crew immediately scurried to their posts or disappeared from sight.

The newcomer stood by as the dark-hooded monk, for such he was, approached Salem and addressed him in a form of Arabic common in North African territories. He first asked Salem what position he had held on his vessel and then inquired after their port of departure and expected destination. He also wished to know what cargo was carried by the ship that had been sunk the previous day by their victorious fleet.

Salem was confident that this final implication was false, a hollow boast, but he feigned a deep sorrow for his fellow seamen. He had replied that he had been assistant navigator and helmsman on the 'sunken' ship and introduced himself as Salem El Sinbad. He could tell by their reaction that his name was of no significance but the navigational knowledge he professed was very welcome to them. When he inquired after the condition of any possible survivors from his lost ship, Salem was told in no uncertain terms that he was not to ask questions, merely to answer promptly and honestly. Salem boldly responded that any sailor not concerned for the wellbeing of his fellow crew men was not worthy of any respect, and informed them that any co-operation expected from him must be reciprocated on their part.

This outburst brought no response, but Salem was then instructed to follow the Leader of the fleet, the Captain and the hooded Monk into the aft cabin. Here, he was shown a map, spread out on the large table in the middle of the spacious cabin, and asked to mark the entire journey of his ship. Salem was interested to note the inaccuracies in the map, which appeared to be the only one in their possession. Browsing through the rest of the documentation, he realised that the production of the map was primitive and based on speculative and unreliable information, rather than the actual charting methods and up-to-date navigational skills that had been available to him. The purpose of the mapping appeared to be the discovery and recording of a navigable route to the Indian sub-continent, by-passing the usual trade routes through the Mediterranean and so allowing for unimpeded and unchallenged mercantile trade.

Salem immediately realised that this knowledge gave him a strong negotiating base with his captors. Through his cloaked interpreter, he pointed out the inaccuracies and missing information in the maps and charts. He was not surprised when the Fleet Leader intervened and indicated that he wished Salem to correct and complete their documentation without delay. Salem responded cautiously that while he was grateful for his rescue from certain death, his rescuers had caused the situation in the first place and therefore his co-operation could only be attained through mutual respect and appropriate status and not as captor and captive.

When they inquired how long it would take to complete the task, he reminded them that it would require him to draw a completely new set of charts and maps from his memory and would therefore take some time. He added that any assistance he received would speed the end result and he repeated that he was willing to help as a fellow seaman and not as a prisoner, and he asked for a promise of safe disembarkation at the first hospitable port.

While they accepted his terms at the time, their sincerity would be judged in due course. For a short period he was still kept in some discomfort but he did notice a subtle change in the attitude of the other sailors and suspected that they had been told by senior officers to accept him as a fellow crew member.

He was awakened early the next morning by a change in the boat's direction. He climbed out into the fresh sea air and as he wandered about the deck he noticed an open hold. Peering in, he saw a huge catapult, the obvious cause of his own ship's mishap and his own demise. He realised from the experience of the previous day, that these people had the knowledge of 'Greek Fire', which he had learnt from his tutors would continue burning even on the water. While he was quite aware of the usefulness of catapults in breaking down defensive walls, he had never before heard of them being used aboard a ship. On looking up, he saw his interpreter beckoning him to the aft castle. Salem ascended the stairs and reached the hooded Monk, who introduced himself as the Padre of the Fleet and the representative of His Holiness the Pope, who had allowed this entire venture to be undertaken by the King of Portugal.

He then proceeded to introduce the Captain and the Navigator. Salem took the opportunity to ask why they had changed direction and was told by the Captain that they were returning to a home port to give a progress report and hopefully to hand-over the upgraded charts, which the Captain hoped Salem would have completed by then.

In stable weather conditions and calm seas, they navigated through the islands at the entrance to the Mozambique Channel. It was early one morning when Salem was deeply involved in his new responsibilities and engrossed in recollecting details of his old charts, when he considered the possibility of attempting to contact his grandfather. He was alone in the chart room and had never before been distracted from his work. With a conscious effort he stretched out his mind to his grandfather. Before long he felt a familiar pattern of thought, a deep concern for his family, from whom he had been separated for so long. Cocooned in an aura of mind control he gently made his presence known to his grandfather.

He saw his grandfather seated on a traditional prayer mat under a jasmine-scented pergola, sipping a glass of bright red aromatic tea.

To Salem's surprise the old gentleman already knew of his boat's arrival and its departure from Aden, but was a little concerned about their most recent progress.

He was very anxious to meet his only grandson for the first time and had been missing his daughter, Bathsheba and his son Yunus, during his long absence from home.

Salem spotted a song-bird perched near Masood and, remembering his experiences with the dolphins, decided to try using the song-bird as a means of communication with his grandfather. The bird seemed at ease in the presence of Masood and soon Salem was in contact with the bird that appeared in a kind of musical rapport with the old man. Salem did not find it difficult to convert his thoughts to coincide with the bird's pattern of song. Masood was taken aback when he heard the bird addressing him by name and realised that he was interpreting the bird's song as human speech. The bird then told him to put aside his concerns for the boat carrying Yunus as it would be arriving in the harbour within the month. All the crew were in good health but were much saddened by the loss of Salem who had fallen overboard and was missing. However, while his fate was unknown to them, he was in fact safe and in good health and spirits.

And so Masood made contact with his Grandson: "*Is that you, Salem, speaking through the medium of the bird? If so, do not withdraw, for I always prayed that another member of my family would inherit the abilities passed down to me from my own Grandfather. This, then, is proof of the belief that the gift often jumps a generation before showing itself again. Do tell me your approximate location, so that I can approach you directly without the medium of the bird as I fear this intervention may traumatise the creature.*"

Salem gently eased himself away from the bird's consciousness without disrupting its song. He then concentrated hard on his present geographic position. Within moments he felt his Grandfather's presence and was aware of a great sense of elation when the old man was confident of his Grandson's well-being.

The conversation proceeded easily: "*Salaam aleykum, my Grandson! It is a joy to see you at last, and very satisfying to see that you are in control of your own destiny. I'm afraid I cannot assist your escape from your present situation, but considering your formidable gifts you are well placed to protect yourself and others and this gives me great comfort. I shall inform your parents and shipmates of your well-being, and I will be observing your progress for as long as I am able, as I have never before been successful in communicating beyond the shores of this vast and beautiful island. You have opened new horizons with your spectacular abilities.*"

"Aleykum Salaam, Grandfather! It is a pleasure joining you and I am honoured to learn that the gift bestowed on me by the Will of Allah, was through you, my Grandfather and our forefathers. I have already contacted my parents on numerous occasions, and informed them of the situation, but cannot guarantee for how much longer I will be able to maintain contact with them due to ever-increasing distance. I believe that you and I together will have greater success. It will be possible for me to learn much from your experience."

"Salem, take some time to consider the philosophy of an older man. The most important lesson any person can teach another is the effective way to question ourselves. The essential knowledge we require for a successful life is already deep within our consciousness, long before we take our first breath. It is built on the experiences passed down to us by our ancestors. We learn from our best tutors how to bring that accumulated learning into use in our everyday life, for our own success and for the advancement of the coming generations. As Nature is infinite, it has the capacity to teach each of us without limitations. While we are alike in so many ways, we also have our differences and even brothers will react to situations and experiences in a different way. I believe you will steer your life well. You will have many experiences that will enhance your relationship with all Nature. I take this opportunity to caution you not to rush headlong into new adventures but always take a wise and calculated approach. May Allah continue to bless you with clear interpretation and prescience throughout your life and ultimately enable you to pass on your very special gifts to grandchildren of your own."

As Salem saw the Padre approaching the cabin door, which he had purposely left ajar, he felt Masood's presence gradually fading.

The Padre was in a formal mood when he informed Salem that the hierarchy aboard had decided to appoint him Assistant Navigator for the duration of the journey to Portugal. When they reached Oporto, the port authorities and other officials would have the power to decide on his future status. He added that Salem could influence his future by the quality of the charts he had been charged to produce. The Padre then offered to teach Salem the Portuguese language and the rites and customs of the Christian religion.

Salem had decided against forming any close relationships during his enforced passage, but he welcomed the assistance offered, for, while he already had a good understanding of the spoken language, the alphabet was totally alien to him. As to the Christian religion, he knew that the Koran el Karim stated that all previous religions were to be respected, for they were all delivered by messengers of God, just like Mohammed himself, and so he would welcome the opportunity to learn more about Christianity. He had already concluded that all religions shared the initial declared objective of improving the lives of ordinary people who needed help against evil, greedy and corrupt excesses. And so he was prepared to learn more.

It was a full cycle of the moon since they had rounded a landmass dominated by a high mountainous plateau and steered their boat north, and twice that time since he had left his father's ship and fellow ship-mates.

As they sailed, he noticed the differing position of the sun in relation to the time of day and concluded that the angle of the sun to the earth varied depending on whether they were travelling north or south. He had learnt another valuable lesson from Nature.

SIX

MYSTERY OF A
NAUTICAL NATURE

On that particular morning the sun had not yet cleared the forested horizon but the daylight was already bright. Salem was on the upper deck taking measurements to confirm their position. He was disturbed by a heavy and eerie silence. He became aware of the absence of the usual birdlife. He knew this was strange as he had noticed they were not far past a fast-flowing river estuary, which would normally have been alive with a wealth of aquatic life and the predatory seagulls such abundance attracted.

He then spotted a lone gull flying high and erratically. He reached out mentally to make contact with the bird in order to discover the reason for this uncanny calm. The bird, which was alarmed and confused, told Salem that there was a huge disturbance in the sea to the south. It appeared like a gigantic, dry river bed in the middle of the sea and it was rolling north at a considerable speed.

Salem, fearing for the safety of his fellows went straight to the Captain, but was only able to describe the danger as a violent and imminent storm. He suggested that they beach the boat on a nearby sandy shore and seek safety on land. The Captain's response was as expected. He ridiculed Salem, believing it to be a simple ruse to facilitate his own escape, and suggested he return to the navigator's room and stay there till called for. Salem, realising the futility of further argument took instant action and dived overboard, hoping to be followed by a recovery party.

The beach was not too far and he was soon wading through shallow waters on a sandy sea-shore. He looked back to see the long boat had been launched and was in hot pursuit.

Salem stayed on the beach long enough to make out that only ten men accompanied the Padre and the second officer in the long-boat. He then made for high ground in full view of his pursuers. On reaching the beach, the Padre led a group in chase, while others pulled the boat high up the beach. Leaving two crew members to guard the boat, the rest followed without fear, as they knew Salem carried no weapons.

When Salem reached the top of the hill, he surveyed the distant horizon for any sign of disaster, but all he saw was a flock of seagulls flying high and fast not stopping to dive for food. The pursuers, more used to life at sea than covering distances on land, were soon exhausted. They were relieved to see that Salem was not running from them and so they slowed down to save their breath and preserve their dignity. On reaching him they saw that Salem was pointing to a flight of birds. Although the birds were flying high they seemed to be peering down at the surface of the ocean. As the sailors followed the gaze of the birds, they saw, to their horrified amazement, there was no water. The ocean appeared dry. It was as if the sea was being sucked away by an invisible giant, leaving a vast 'nothingness', about 400 arm spans wide but endless in length, and travelling relentlessly at the speed of a galloping horse, towards the ship they had so recently left. Where the sea had been one moment, only rocks and sand were visible for the next thirty seconds and then, miraculously the calm water returned. There was no immediate evidence of this phenomenon, and they may not have noticed it, had it not been for the strange reaction of the gulls. But changes had taken place! The ship they had left, not so long ago, and had been calmly awaiting their return, was suddenly sighted, perched on a large rock at an unnatural angle. Even as they watched, it disappeared slowly from their sight without leaving a trace. Salem estimated that the depth of water at that point was about two hundred feet.

The sailors stood transfixed with fear for the lives of their fellow crewmen still aboard the ship, and none would have believed it had they not witnessed it with their own eyes. Nothing in their previous lives had prepared them for such an event.

Salem felt the presence of an enormous force of Nature passing over the land and sea. And once again he was conscious of the power of Nature beyond Man's comprehension.

Both the Second Officer and the Padre appeared traumatised by the experience and their minds and expressions were blank. Gradually their vision cleared and the Padre turned to Salem with an enquiring look.

Salem realised that an explanation was necessary, but he carefully adapted his story to the Padre's beliefs. He said, "The Holy Mary appeared to me in my sleep last night and warned me of this coming disaster, instructing me to save my fellow sailors. When the Captain ignored my warning, I decided on the course of action I took and it appears to have saved the lives of thirteen people."

Turning his attention to the sea, Salem saw that the group of sailors that had been left on the shore guarding the long boat were looking up towards them, but on their knees, as in prayer. The Padre, wondering at this behaviour, ran down to the shore to investigate. Following the sailors' gaze, he looked back towards the hill and had to shield his eyes. The sun had cleared the horizon, but seemed to be nestling behind a small white cloud, its rays forming a glowing halo above Salem's head.

Salem, realising how his appearance was being interpreted by the sailors, decided to use this new respect to his advantage. He knew that in the circumstances their best chance of success was strong leadership and a disciplined line of command. He immediately took control of the group with the Padre as his confidante and the Second officer in charge of the sailors. The long boat was equipped with a sail, as well as some emergency provisions including a small barrel of water and a large wineskin. Salem instructed Carlos, the Second Officer, to give everyone a good mouthful of wine, in celebration of their survival and then empty the wineskin, to allow them to carry a maximum quantity of water. Two groups were organised to search for fresh water and fruit, enough for all for a minimum of ten days sailing. He explained to his fellows that while he expected a period of sailing along the present fertile coast, they would encounter a desolate area where it would be impossible to replenish their supplies and therefore all rations would have to be carefully controlled. He also explained that as they had no commodities aboard that could be used for barter, they could not be sure of a friendly reception by native people.

The foragers returned after a couple of hours, laden with water, an assortment of fruit and bringing with them a near-naked, black-skinned young girl in her early teens. She was not in any way distressed with her new company and was striding along comfortably balancing a large bunch of bananas on her head. Carlos appeared to have used his rank to lay claim on the girl. Salem recognised some Arabic in her speech but was unable to fully understand her language. At first he used sign language and some mental probing until he eventually found that he could follow her conversation without understanding the actual words. She talked about her village, which was about an hour's walk along the river into the forest, and about her family tribe. When Salem became more familiar with her speech he was able to ask her if she had ever seen other strangers like themselves. She told him of men who had come to barter for the shiny metal the villagers found along the river banks. They would collect the fragments together in a large container and heat them until they melted, then cooled the liquid to form a large block. The metal was soft so they could not use it for tools, but it was bright and shiny and did not rust. The strangers came from a place they called Dakar and they were different in appearance from the sailors she had now met. To trade they had brought along clothes and some materials not known in the village. They arrived in a large boat and they carried weapons to punish villagers that did not obey them. Salem translated her story for his men, taking care to leave out any reference to the 'shiny metal', which he guessed was gold. He had no intention of tempting his sailors to go off seeking for gold with nothing to barter with and only violence as a means of acquiring it. Then he asked Carlos to remove the highly decorated coat he was wearing and offer it to the girl as a parting gift. When he explained to Carlos that a long boat was no place for a lone young girl, among so many men, he noticed that Carlos's obvious sadness was matched by the Padre's smile of approval. But Salem understood Carlos's disappointment and tried to console him by suggesting that the girl would cherish that special present for the rest of her life and the memory of that should keep any man warm on a cold and lonely night.

The girl, herself, appeared dejected when she realised that she was to be left behind, but she readily accepted the gift of the jacket. She donned it with pride and pulled it snugly around her, covering her breasts which, until then, had been boldly naked- to the great admiration of the onlookers. She stood there, knee-deep in the shallows as they pushed the boat into the yawning water and out into the swell, before hoisting the mainsail. The oarsmen helped speed the departure, by rowing until the sail was filled by the southerly afternoon breeze. She held up her arms in farewell, until the oarsmen lifted all five pairs of oars in salute to her as they rounded the headland and disappeared from her view.

That night the exhausted sailors dropped off to sleep without leaving their benches. A few slipped down to rest their heads against the side of the boat, but observing them Salem realised that none of them was comfortable.

Carlos agreed to stay at the helm while Salem went to join the Padre. He found his friend staring at the infinity of a star-filled night sky, in a state of deep meditation. Sensing Salem's presence, he shook himself out of his reverie and quietly shared with Salem his surprise at the many strange things he had recently witnessed. He questioned Salem's ability to communicate with people in the jungle, his unique understanding of the ways of Nature, of the Oceans, and the night sky. He said that after seeing the vision of Salem on the mountain, he realised that Salem had been chosen by the holy Virgin Mary, to be a messenger to her people, and therefore must be a saint among men. Salem, anxious not to be seen as too extra-ordinary, explained his knowledge in terms of his study of astronomy. His understanding of language he attributed to the guidance of a well-travelled and wise father. As to being chosen for the task of messenger, he exclaimed that no one could interpret the ways of the Holy Ones and before the Padre could respond, he quickly changed the subject by pointing to various constellations and identifying those stars which were particularly useful in navigation.

The Padre had a deep understanding of the teachings in the Bible, which he believed was the source of all learning, but he was intelligent and sought wider information. He was impressed by Salem's knowledge and assured him that he would be a willing student, were Salem prepared to teach him more about the heavens. Salem replied that although he was not a trained teacher and still learning himself, as he believed that one gathers knowledge and understanding every moment of life, he would certainly welcome the Padre as a friend and fellow student in the journey that lay ahead.

They lowered themselves into the bottom of the boat with their heads resting against the side. The calm movement of the boat reflected the gentle waves and the warm night air lulled them into a relaxed state.

Before long the Padre's throaty, husky snores indicated a deep sleep, while Salem's thoughts turned again to the young girl from the forest. His mind found her and gradually he eased into her thoughts. He was surprised how different her daily life was from his. Considering the challenges that Nature placed on her remote community, her daily routine could not be considered monotonous. The tribe's acceptance of their life experiences, with many less taboos than Salem was familiar with in similar primitive cultures, was noteworthy.

Salem remembered describing her as an innocent young girl although he was in no position to assess her sexual maturity. His own knowledge in those matters was limited to a lesson from his tutor just after his thirteenth birthday. His actual experience was confined to an unexplained emotional and physical arousal when he was engaged in a game of wrestling with a young girl in the harem. That physical contact was the first he could recollect with a female outside of his immediate family. He remembered later, wishing that the contact would last for ever, although he did not understand why this should be. However, he was still painfully aware that if there was an innocent around it was almost certainly himself, and possibly also the Padre.

It was about two hours to day-break, all were asleep except Salem. He had taken control of the tiller which was held securely between his legs. Only the small forward sail was necessary, due to a strong current that was propelling them northward towards their destination. The solitary desolation of the moment caused his mind to wander in search of the village in the jungle and the hut where the young girl lived. Salem psychically encountered the girl asleep in one of the small wooden huts near the centre of a small clearing almost hidden by the surrounding tall trees. His heart beat faster as he watched her sleeping, her body twisting and turning as she dreamt. Emboldened by his own desire, Salem probed gently into her subconscious mind and found to his surprise that he was the subject of her sexual fantasy. Salem feared disturbing her and thereby losing the chance to stay with her and participate in her dream. He found the very real experience exhilarating and yet he was more fatigued than he had ever felt. His body tingled with excitement as a chill ran down his spine. Eventually he took control of his breathing and physically and mentally calmed down. As he gradually detached his mind from her and slowly drifted away from her presence, she reached out towards the wall and handed him a primitive, woven picture with some trinkets attached to it.

Quite suddenly he was wide awake. The sun was clearing the shoreline in a glorious, red-orange glow that lit up the wisps of cloud in the sky, the leaves in the distant forest and the waves on the sea. His attention turned immediately to his imminent duties. Without thinking he slipped his hand into his pocket, and shivered in disbelief as it closed on a small woven square.

Realising the magnitude and implications of the night's events left Salem unsettled. His fear and apprehension grew as he became aware that his psychic gifts were far greater than he had previously understood. Not only could he converse with animals and birds; conduct mind to mind conversations with people at a distance; remotely view distant people and places as he had with his grandfather; but now he understood that what he had just witnessed was beyond even an 'out of body' experience. He had, apparently been in two places at the same time. In some way his body had accompanied his spirit to the girl's home and he held tangible evidence of this. He had crossed the line into another dimension!

Feeling thoroughly shaken by this discovery, he needed the calming effect of contact with his parents. Taking advantage of the early hour, while his ship-mates were still sleeping, he sought messages from his parents and grandfather. Knowing that his grandfather had suffered loneliness, he was reassured and delighted to hear that Yunus, Rashid and the remaining crew had reached his grandfather on the previous day and all were in good health and the ship and cargo were safe and unharmed.

From time to time, Salem had spotted other craft along the shoreline. They were long and narrow with a tall, single sail. Being shallow and fast they were built for inshore waters and were unsteady on the open sea. The presence of these boats suggested the proximity of populated land. Salem scanned the distant shoreline for evidence of this and finding a few scattered tribes he sent out his mind to probe these native people for information. He learnt that most were not Heathen, but had already been converted to Islam and could converse reasonably well in Arabic. However, he also learnt that Spanish and Portuguese traders had visited the shores and having demonstrated their powers of destruction had made no friends among the inhabitants.

Salem, fearing an attack, altered their direction and sailed further out to the open sea.

SEVEN

THE DOLDRUMS

With the loss of their ship and fellow ship-mates and the consequent lack of meaningful activity on board the long-boat, a deep depression set in among the crew and it taxed even the consoling powers of the Padre to keep their spirits up. Salem had taken his turn in rowing the boat, partly to establish himself as a regular member of the crew but also to provide his much needed exercise. Remembering his father's teaching on the importance of the balance in body and mind and also the symmetry of the body, he would alternate between port and starboard.

Using his ability to read into the minds of others, he was able to forecast their emotional difficulties, and while he did not feel he had the experience to deal with these problems himself he was able to bring them to the notice of the very able Padre. The Padre's patience and skill appeared endless and this prevented any potential friction on board in their stressful circumstances.

It was not long before everyone realised that this was to be a lengthy and frustrating journey. Salem felt that, perhaps, he was the least prepared to endure the privations of life on a small boat on the high seas. In spite of his father's rigorous training, the actual experiences of all the others had prepared them better to cope with the difficulties they would most certainly encounter. At least the others could look forward to a joyful re-union with loved ones at the end of their ordeal. This was not a pleasure he could anticipate for many months to come. In spite of this, he accepted that he would be the main instrument of their survival and a successful end to their journey.

One windless day, when the men were totally exhausted and listless with boredom, a sailor started reminiscing about the girl they had left behind. He suggested, somewhat lewdly, how things could have been improved had she been with them. He persisted in picturesque descriptions, to the enthusiastic approval of some of the sailors. But his comments raised deep anger and embarrassment in Carlos, who appeared to be on the verge of violence. In an attempt to defuse the situation, Salem rose and loudly began to recall a story he felt was more suitable to the occasion.

"Once upon a time there was a Sultan of exceptional reputation, for he always showed admirable judgements in all his decisions, particularly those involving the problems of ordinary people. His wisdom was beyond compare. Everyone respected him and many loved him. Among those he loved there was one great favourite, his falcon, who was his faithful companion whenever he ventured from the Palace. On one such occasion, on a hunting expedition into the desert, accompanied by his usual entourage of noblemen and guards, the Sultan, due to the superior speed of his magnificent horse, became separated from the rest of the party. No-one was over-concerned as they knew they could follow the horse's hoof-prints in the sand and would eventually find the horse tethered with the Sultan resting nearby, with his faithful falcon perched proudly on his forearm. However, on that particular occasion, an unexpected and violent sand-storm rose and hid everything from view. It lasted less than an hour but the desert sand and fine dust that it raised, lingered for much longer. It was not long before the Sultan realised how much he relied on others for essential provisions. The water in the small bottle he carried was totally inadequate for his parched throat.

In a short time his thirst became unbearable but his first thought was for his beloved falcon and he removed the hood from the falcon's head so that the bird might be free to provide for itself.

As the dust gradually settled, he saw in the distance a large rocky outcrop. Recognising it as a distinctive landmark, he decided to seek its shelter. Conscious that he would be frantic in this hostile terrain without his horse, he coaxed the animal slowly towards the rock to avoid unnecessary exhaustion. After what felt like eternity, he reached the base of a sheer rock that seemed to reach up to the sky. Before the Sultan had a chance to dismount, his poor horse collapsed to the sand, nearly trapping the Sultan's leg beneath its exhausted body. The Sultan left the animal lying and started scrambling round the rock looking for a track, to climb to a vantage point. To his amazement he noticed a droplet of water that appeared to have fallen from the heavens. It was a tiny amount but he was desperate and eagerly undid the golden cap and placed his water flask under the droplets in the hope of collecting enough to quench his thirst. The drips were slow, but eventually the vessel held a mouthful, enough, at least, to moisten his aching throat. He was already kneeling before the flask, as if in prayer. He reached out towards it but before he could grasp it his falcon appeared from nowhere and, with the end of its wing, knocked over the flask, spilling the precious contents into the scorching sand.

The Sultan's frustration was contained in the prayers he said to calm his frayed nerves, before he replaced the flask in the hope of re-filling it. This time the drips appeared even slower, possibly due to his heightened state of despair. With no alternative, he settled down in the shade of the rock to wait and meanwhile prayed to Allah for his safe return to his family and friends. This time, he reached for the flask with hardly a mouthful in it, but again, before he could put it to his lips the falcon appeared and knocked it from his hand. The Sultan, in an uncontrollable rage, grabbed the bird and ended the life of his long-time friend and companion by wringing its neck.

The next moment, with tears streaming down his face, he stood distraught, for not only had he lost his faithful falcon but the precious droplets had stopped flowing. He had to climb the rock and find the source of the water. He discovered some foot-holds carved in the rock and, eventually, with his last ounce of stamina, reached the top. At the peak, he froze in terror. Before him, lay an old dragon, deep in sleep. The huge mouth was half open and drops of saliva dripped on to the tufts of desert scrub on which he lay. The Sultan watched in horror, as the tufts withered instantly at the touch of the saliva. He was immediately filled with overwhelming remorse for killing his falcon that had been faithful to the end and had undoubtedly saved his master from almost certain death. He saw then that the gold of his flask had masked the poison of the dragon's saliva. Carefully avoiding disturbing the dragon, the Sultan explored the small plateau on the top of the rock and managed to find a little vegetation that had been fed by the scant moisture from the rare atmosphere. He gathered a handful and chewed gratefully, happy to soothe the roughness of his throat, if only a little, before starting his descent. He returned to the place where he had left his horse and to his surprise found the beast recovered from its exhaustion and standing, patiently awaiting the return of his master. As the Sultan mounted he heard the sound of horses and turned to see the welcome sight of his entourage approaching him at full gallop. It turned out they had spotted the reflection of the many medals on his attire as he was climbing the peak of the rock. Everyone was relieved and happy at the timely re-union, but the sultan chose not to explain the absence of his falcon. That would be a lesson for him to remember for the rest of his life."

The sailors listened to Salem's story in silence and the hush continued as they wrestled with the moral that loyal friends are worthy of trust however the circumstances may indicate the contrary. Gradually they all dozed off and Salem was left alone trying hard to remember where he had heard that story before.

They were sailing past a vast expanse of desert, with no means of replenishing their diminishing stores. Fortunately, thanks to an unusually heavy rainfall they had, at least, been able to restore their dwindling water supply. The fishing was not plentiful but adequate for their needs, so they were in no risk of starvation. They were making good progress. The wind had dropped out over the last three days and the oarsmen were taking it easy as the boat was being swept along by a strong northerly current just beneath the surface of the sea.

Salem now had some serious decisions ahead. He knew that his sailors would be desperate for time on land. They had been at sea in precarious situations for many weeks and they longed to join old friends and carouse in the taverns of the harbours along their route. But Salem knew that sailors were not known for their moderation and would often become drunk and boisterous, regularly getting into fights and brawls with each other and also local people. He also knew that many ports along the coast of Africa would not be welcoming to Christian sailors and they might find a very hostile reception. Anxious to avoid this he consulted his friends, the Padre and Carlos. From his navigation he estimated they were about two days sailing from a port called Casa-Blanco or White City, as the locals called it. He knew it to be an Islamic city of the Moors and while he could expect a warm welcome, his Christian companions would not be so well received, due to regular ransacking by nearby Christian countries. Another five days sailing to the northeast would bring them to a group of islands, which he understood to be in the control of the Spanish king, and he was not in a position to judge their reception in advance. However, another option would be to continue their journey for a further ten days with the possibility of reaching the home shores of Portugal. Each choice had its dangers but finally both the Padre and Carlos appreciated Salem's dilemma and all three agreed that it would be best to continue their voyage to Portugal. Carlos and the Padre accepted the responsibility of explaining the circumstances and the decision to the crew. In spite of their disappointment at the loss of possibly imminent shore leave the crew were resigned and relieved that they were not so far from home.

When the fore-watch shouted, 'Ship-Ahoy' and pointed to the northwest, a great cheer went up from the sailors, who stood on their benches and waved their oars as high as possible above their heads. Some even lost their balance in their enthusiasm, toppling into the water, only to be hauled out dripping by their laughing friends. The reason for their joy was a ship similar to their own, but Salem was apprehensive. He tried to restrain their enthusiasm with the help of the Padre and after some initial hesitation Carlos became aware of Salem's ill ease and joined the two of them. But the sailors were beyond curbing their celebrations and resisted all attempts to calm them.

Salem decided that detection was unavoidable and avoidance impossible so all three counsellors accepted their impending fate with a grim smile, which was greeted by the sailors with another innocent cheer.

It was clear that they had been spotted by the foreign ship, when it was seen to change its direction and steer straight towards the long-boat. Anxious to keep his crew as calm as possible, Salem did not share his alarm when he noticed the absence of a flag of national origin on the approaching vessel. For him this could mean only one thing and he feared for their fate.

The crew, oblivious of the signs, were in high spirits when the ship pulled alongside and threw them a line.

Once on board, they found their rescuers to be mainly French but, by the varied and colourful attire and the sound of many languages spoken, it was clear the crew was drawn from all over the Mediterranean region.

EIGHT

THE PIRATES

They were indeed pirates, with no affiliation to anyone but their Captain and themselves. The Captain was seated on a comfortable, highly decorated chair fixed to the aft deck. He was dressed in finery, embroidered with gold and silk, more in keeping with an aristocrat or a high ranking military officer, than for combat on the high seas. Salem immediately judged from his attitude and bearing that he was intelligent and well-respected.

As soon as they were on board, Salem and the Padre were taken before the Captain, while the rest of the crew were ushered below deck without delay. When questioned, the Padre described himself as the spiritual leader on a sea venture, commissioned by the King of Portugal. Unfortunately their ship had been lost in a freak of nature. The men on the long boat were the only survivors and were on their way back to Lisbon. The captain nodded towards Salem and the Padre introduced him as Simon, a name that would disguise his eastern origins and which he could readily accept, and explained that he was the navigator aboard the ship-wrecked vessel.

The Captain soon realised that the passengers he had acquired could be quite profitable to him. He was aware of the King of Portugal's desire to find new trading routes to the East, avoiding the necessity to pay homage or taxes to Venice or Genoa. By-passing these two dominating powers in the Mediterranean Sea was a long-standing ambition of France and Spain. If this young navigator had any information to this end, he could be a very valuable trading commodity in himself.

The Captain raised himself from his chair and beckoned Simon to follow him to his cabin. At the same time Simon noticed that the Padre was being taken below deck to what turned out to be very uncomfortable conditions. It was quite obvious that, while there was always room for willing and able-bodied men on board ship, a priest, particularly one loyal to his King as well as his God was of no asset to the Captain or the ship.

On entering the cabin, the Captain told Simon that his name was Pierre and confirmed, as Simon had suspected, that he was originally from France. He was anxious to learn more from the navigator and, as on another occasion, Simon was told that his well-being would be proportional to his co-operation. This was exactly what Simon was expecting and he readily accepted Pierre's conditions and offered him complete and unreserved support.

Pierre seemed satisfied with this, but Simon guessed that the Pirate leader had deeper intentions than he had shown. He suspected that he had interests that would take him further east than Portugal or even the coast of Spain and this could be advantageous for Simon's own plans.

They entered the Mediterranean Sea early one morning and Simon had spent a long period in communication with his parents. He discussed with Sinbad the time differences between their two locations, and the alteration in the sun's elevation that he had witnessed when in contact with his grandfather and the puzzle that these observations had created in his calculations. In an attempt to solve this conundrum he had concluded that maybe the earth was round. In reply Sinbad showed no surprise and explained that all experienced sailors allowed for a curvature in order to calculate a more accurate position. Simon judged the time premature to make known the theory that he had shared only with his father. He decided to wait and carry out further investigations, so that he might use his findings to his greatest advantage.

Pierre was four or five years older than Simon and although he had a relaxed command of his men and an authority he must have acquired at a young age, Simon guessed he had limited experience in life at sea.

History was in the making! Pierre was aware that a third crusade was being planned. The Man with the Fisherman's Ring had sent his emissaries to all the great houses of Christendom requesting their support for this venture. This could provide great opportunities for anyone with an entrepreneurial spirit. Simon felt certain that very soon he would be involved, with Pierre, in a great requisitioning of vessels to carry large numbers of men and supportive supplies and that the providers of this armada would be made very rich. After the mayhem and destruction that had been experienced across Europe as a direct result of the previous two crusades, many Christians doubted the claims of holiness made by the various transient armies and detested the ravages caused on their lands. Pierre, being aware of this and clear-thinking, had seen an alternative and sought to influence the tacticians at an early stage of the planning. It was also important that he convince his elder brother, Philip. Pierre realised that he could trust Simon and by confiding in him, could only benefit from the relationship.

Pierre was resting in his armchair on the aft deck, watching his crew at their tasks. He turned away from them to address Simon who was leaning on the balustrade admiring the sunset. He knew that the time was right to acquaint Simon with his true background. His opening remark surprised Simon.

"Simon, you must know that I am Pierre, the younger brother of King Philip of Paris and Spain!"

He went on to explain that he had run away to sea before his brother was crowned King, in order to avoid conflict or any complications. He was vastly in debt to a friend for loaning him the fine vessel in which they sailed and also to the Duke of Bordeaux for his financial support. He went on to explain further that he had always enjoyed the support and loyalty of the elite officers in the Palace Guard. From a young age his ambition had been to join the Military and his education had been geared to the science of war, whereas Philip had a good understanding of engineering, but he was always more contemplative and religious and had natural statesmanship. Philip's devotion to religion made him the favourite of the Cardinal and the

Pope and being the elder brother made him the natural heir to the throne of France. However, Philip feared possible challenges to his rule, because of Pierre's popularity with the senior army officers. Realising that this could put Pierre in danger, his friends had recommended a spell of diplomatic absence. This had led to Pierre's departure with a number of the loyal officers who had followed him into voluntary exile and were serving on the ship.

Pierre, anxious to be reconciled with his brother and prove his loyalty, was working on a number of plans. Philip had agreed to the betrothal of their sister, Princess Alice to his childhood friend, Richard Coeur de Lion, with a gift of the district of Vexing as a dowry. This arrangement not only increased the bond of the two powerful friends, but formed an alliance stronger than any in Christendom. It was also known that the Pope did not favour Charlemagne for the next Holy Roman Emperor and Pierre believed that with only a little encouragement in certain areas, Philip could be placed in an advantageous position to be considered for this distinction.

Meanwhile, Pierre continued to expand his plan to exercise his influence on his contacts in France and Genoa, encouraging them to commit their substantial fleets to the transportation of Crusading armies to the Holy Land, in exchange for a considerable sum for their passage.

One problem that Pierre could foresee when confronting his brother, was convincing him that he had no ulterior motive for his business plan, apart from his stated intentions to provide a service and secure financial profit. His major difficulty in maximizing his scheme, however, would be with the two competing Republica

Marinas, as he would have to encourage Venice to participate in the venture alongside their age-old rival Genoa. Simon would be made responsible for convincing these two powerful maritime cities, who, for a very long time had held the monopoly of trade with the East and so had accrued massive wealth and political influence, that Spain and Portugal were now a potential threat to them.

Pierre suggested that he and Simon should travel to Rome where they would seek an audience with the Pope and ask for his blessing on their venture and his nomination as organiser of the official acquisition of the armada. Pierre hoped that this action would lead to his brother's approval.

The ship they were travelling on would be prepared for the ambassadorial task. It was to be scrubbed and painted and even an appropriate standard was prepared to replace the already discarded pirate flag. Pierre's friend, the Duke of Bordeaux, would prepare the necessary documents of introduction to the Holy See.

Simon saw this as an opportunity to help his friend the Padre. He suggested that, in the light of the religious nature of their mission, Pierre might deem it appropriate to reconsider the position of the Padre and re-instate him to religious duties on board.

NINE

ROME AND BEYOND

At first sight, Rome appeared very like the Baghdad Simon had learned about in his early studies. It was a religious and cultural centre, built on both banks of a river. The main difference was that, while Baghdad's river, the Tigris, was navigable to the city and beyond, Rome could not be reached by any sizeable vessel. The Tevere or Tiberius was fast-running, especially in the rainy season, but it carried much silt from the mountains, and so was shallow, even as it reached the sea. Rome was only accessible by road. However, unlike Baghdad, whose road system was poor, Rome could be reached by road from all parts of the country. Ostia had served as a harbour for Rome throughout its history, supplying grain from the extensively farmed North African territories, where vast areas of forest had been cleared for its cultivation. Ostia was linked to the capital city by an outstanding paved road, lined for its entire length with magnificent evergreen cedars and cypress trees, lending shade to both freight and pedestrians.

Immediately on arrival, Pierre sent a messenger with

his credentials and a hint as to the urgency of the matter, to the Vatican, in expectation of being granted an audience with the Pope. He was gratified to receive a prompt and favourable response and a time was set for the reception of his delegation after lunch on the next day.

Pierre and his faithful friends, dressed in the finery befitting their rank, formed an impressive entourage, as they proceeded towards Rome with their Vatican escorts.

Simon, himself, had dressed with care. He had been given access to Pierre's wardrobe and had selected garments modestly for his visit to the city, choosing, for sentimental reasons, to add the short-sleeved coat his mother had so lovingly sewn for him. As a Muslim, he had not been included in the Vatican party, and so decided to take a leisurely stroll around the city. He found himself in a western metropolis far larger than he could ever have imagined. He was astonished at the sheer size of the population on the streets and of its ethnic variety. This left him pondering on what might induce so many people to live together in such close proximity. He considered the logistical difficulties of even providing the daily requirements for such a large and eclectic group. He could imagine no reason for this way of life but realised that people do not necessarily need a reason for their behaviour and may be the pawns of circumstances rather than logic.

He was shocked at the devastation of natural land and forest to provide the space and building materials for such a huge city. Looking around him he was convinced that not everyone shared equally in the benefits that were provided. Eventually he found himself amongst a crowd in a market-place. This was more familiar to him. It was only in the dress of the traders and their customers that the scene differed from the markets he had visited as a child in Basra.

Moving between the stalls he noticed a young lady stumbling into an elderly gentleman who was unbalanced by the unexpected contact. Simon was close enough to attempt to assist them both. As he moved to do so, he saw the young woman removing a small purse from the cord that held the gentleman's garment. She turned slightly to hand the purse to a large, athletic-looking man who happened to be passing at that moment, at the same time apologising to the gentleman for her clumsiness and trying to escape from the entanglement. Simon slipped behind the retreating girl who tripped against him, giving him the opportunity to snatch the purse before the accomplice's hand closed on it. However, the large man's hand did not go empty as he closed his grip on Simon's wrist. Simon reacted instinctively by ducking under the restraining arm and spinning the massive body into a somersault that left it sprawled on the cobblestones. The disturbance had caused bystanders to hurry away, anxious not to be drawn into the fray, and a clearing formed around the combatants, drawing the attention of the city guards. Simon indicated to his two adversaries to leave without delay as he had no desire to attract further attention to himself.

Simon hurried to the old gentleman, who, in his bewilderment did not immediately recognise the purse which Simon offered him, but accepted it with surprise and delight when he realised what had happened. He introduced himself as Signor Baggio from Genoa and opened his returned purse with the intention of offering Simon a reward for his honesty, but Simon politely declined. After introducing himself, Simon explained to the gentleman that he was a stranger and would be delighted if he could share his company for a while and so learn more of the wonderful city around him. Signor Baggio declared that he also was not a native of Rome, but had, in fact, lived there for a number of years. His family was from Genoa but they had maintained a residence in Rome for a very long time as he, and his father before him, had been representatives for Genoa in the Vatican State. He had been on his way home when he was attacked and as he was still quite shaken he would be pleased for the company and would gladly show the young man such sights as fell on their route. He then invited Simon to join him for lunch at his villa. Simon thanked the Signor for his hospitality and accepted the invitation with enthusiasm. He recognised this as an opportunity to also learn more about the Signor's home city of Genoa which had been brought to his attention so recently. Their journey through the city took a great deal longer than either had anticipated. Signor Baggio, his previous bad experience soon forgotten, wandered around happily, with Simon alongside him, each enjoying the other's company and a mutual enthusiasm. Simon was fascinated as the old gentleman expounded on the extra-ordinary talents and skills of the numerous, distinguished men, who had made their mark on that outstanding city with its unique and ancient culture.

Eventually they arrived at the residence, tired and hungry. A heavily decorated door was built into a sturdy, high wall, which obscured any view of the property from the street. The Signor opened the door with a large brass key and stood back for his guest to enter. Simon was aghast at the contrast with the majority of the dwellings that he had seen nearby. He found himself standing in a beautifully designed and well maintained garden. Bushes, trees and an abundance of colourful flowers lined the raised, paved pathway, which opened into a wide circle in front of an imposing house. In the centre of the circle an exquisitely carved marble fountain played, with statues and sculptures visible through the cascading waters. The house was approached by a set of four marble steps which fanned down from the door to the courtyard. The stairway was covered to form a large porch-way which was supported by two marble columns at the furthest ends. This gave protection from rain and sun. The stonework of the house showed the art of masonry at its best. This was undoubtedly the home of a wealthy and influential man.

Simon fell behind his host as he followed him up the steps to the entrance. On seeing them, a number of servants hurried to greet them, expressing their concern at their master's unexpected delay. Signor Baggio acknowledged them by asking that the food be served immediately in the rear garden under the lilac tree.

After washing his hands, as was his custom, Simon took his seat among the comfortable cushions on a long low couch, beneath the fragrant lilac blossom. Many garden birds drank and splashed in a nearby fountain, entertaining the Signor, who was already seated and awaiting his guest. As he had noted on entering the property, the garden he was now in was also cleverly designed for symmetry and balance. The taller growth around the perimeter wall gave a feeling of privacy and seclusion. Geometric flower beds filled with plants of graded heights, faced in towards the central fountain. The lilac tree providing their shade was the only exception to this order. The whole effect was one of restfulness and peace.

Simon had been made aware that table etiquette in western cities was very different from that in his own home. He had watched Pierre and copied his movements and manners, and so on this occasion, even though, by now he was very hungry, he watched the Signor and allowed him to start his meal first. He found the food excellent. The fruit was fresh, ripe and tasty and the bread freshly baked from well-sifted wheat. The cheese had a very agreeable after-taste and appeared to have matured for a long time in close proximity to a variety of strong and sweet-smelling herbs. Simon also enjoyed the partially crushed green olives that had been mixed with chopped garlic, crushed coriander seeds and thinly sliced bitter orange, all moistened with a little olive oil. When he declined the wine offered to him he was brought clear spring water. At first the conversation focussed on Simon's travels that had led him to the city of Rome. Tactfully he avoided mentioning the period of his life before he joined the Portuguese vessel. He described himself as the young navigator, who had suffered unfortunate circumstances on a journey of discovery, sponsored by the King of Portugal. Simon explained that he, and a number of other lucky sailors, had been rescued by a French Nobleman, who was the captain of a vessel. He told his host that his captain was in Rome and on his way to Vatican City for an audience with His Holiness, the Pope. He declared himself happy to be in such excellent company on his first shore leave. Everything was far beyond his expectations. Signor Baggio listened to Simon's story without interruption. His interest increased with every sentence uttered. He suggested their conversation continue after a short siesta, as it was his custom to take a rest after his midday meal. A young and attractive girl approached them with moistened towels and Simon followed his host in accepting one. As she left them the Signor mentioned that she was the daughter of the cook and was employed as his chamber maid.

Simon was as ready for a rest as his host, but before surrendering himself to slumber he decided to use his special skills to seek for more knowledge of his host. While lying on the couch feigning sleep, he allowed his awareness to drift into the building. The interior of the house showed a home of considerable opulence, decorated with the taste that prosperity allowed. It was a home where culture balanced wealth. The lower part of the building housed a large and well-appointed bathing area and a well-designed kitchen with sufficient facilities to cater for a very large number of diners. It was obvious from the many sculptures and paintings depicting incidents at sea that the family had close and long-standing marine interests, but these appeared more related to acquiring wealth than to naval battles.

When his mind entered the master's chambers Simon encountered the pretty servant girl leaning by the window watching two sleeping men below. He realised that it was actually himself that she was watching. As he eased himself into her consciousness, he found her daydreaming of the man she loved. Interpreting her thoughts, he was interested to find that she had enjoyed a relationship with the gardener, which she had kept secret for three years. Hesitant to become more involved in her fantasies he gradually withdrew, but could not avoid a shiver of titillation at the prospect of further voyeurism. Mentally returning to his reclining body he allowed both mind and body to relax into complete rest, as he found the day's activities had totally sapped his resources.

On sensing his host's awakening, Simon also opened his eyes, and rising from his seat, he thanked the Signor for his excellent hospitality. Signor Baggio, in return, told Simon he had very much enjoyed his acquaintance. He confirmed that his position in the city of Rome was that of Consul for Genoa, and if Monsieur Pierre wished to further his ambitions, he would be welcome at his home and he would be happy to assist him.

Signor Baggio then asked for writing materials to be brought and he drew up a document declaring Simon to be a privileged and protected person by order of the Consul of Genoa. He included an invitation for both Simon and Pierre to join him for lunch the following day.

When Simon was finally ready to leave, the Signor offered him the company of one of his servants to escort him through the maze of city streets. Simon's first instinct was to decline but then curiosity about the gardener, whom he believed was the young girl's lover, made him suggest the gardener as a guide. He reasoned that it would be an opportunity for him to discuss the intricacies of laying a fine garden. Signor Baggio smiled, telling Simon that the gardener was very old with a missing leg and the long walk would be arduous for him and maybe next time he visited, Entrée would be glad to find time to discuss his mastery of gardens. This astonished Simon and thanking the Signor again he set off to make his own way back to his ship.

It was time for dinner that evening when Simon eventually arrived, and Pierre invited him to join him and fellow officers in the Captain's cabin. Dinner had apparently been held for his arrival and the anti-pasta was already on the table. Pierre was most anxious to share with Simon an account of the day's events. He had met with His Holiness at the Vatican and Pope Gregory appeared to be in complete agreement with Pierre over the preference of sea transport for the Crusaders. The Pope was not oblivious to the loss of Faith of those who had suffered, for many years, at the hands of marauding Crusaders, ransacking and commandeering excessive provisions, as they travelled through Christian territories, on their way to the Kingdom of Rum in Byzantium.

The Pope, seeing a way to put a stop to this vandalism and restore respect for the Church, gladly appointed Pierre to be responsible for organising this alternative transport of armies to the Holy Land. He had his secretariat prepare all necessary documentation, which he duly signed and sealed, before handing it to Pierre as recommendation to all the Great Houses in Christendom.

The Second Crusade had not gone well. The previous Pope, Urban 3rd had grieved on his deathbed over the defeat of Guy de Lusignan of Jerusalem at the Battle of Tiberius, five years earlier. Then just three months later, Jerusalem, followed by Tripoli and Tyre, fell to Saladin. And so Saladin conquered the Holy Land and ended the

Frankish Kingdom in the Levant. A final blow was struck when Saladin took possession of the 'Fragment of the Holy Cross', which was regarded by all Christians to be the holiest of all relics. This sacrilege had to be avenged, regardless of the fact that it had not been damaged and all Christians were free to visit it at all times, without hindrance. The act itself provided the Pope with sufficient justification for a third crusade.

Pierre assessed the leaders who might take advantage of his ships. One possible omission would be Frederic Barbarossa, the Holy Roman Emperor and King of Germany, who had declared himself Commander in Chief of all the Christian armies. He always chose his own ways of doing things, which was one of the many reasons for his unpopularity. Apparently, Frederic had already made preparations for his army to march overland by way of Asia Minor. While Pierre had been given the Papal blessing to arrange the logistics of the project and to rally all the noble Christian houses, he still had the problem of finding the substantial funding required for the venture. He would be receiving an amount from the Vatican before his departure, which would cover some of his initial expenditure, but raising the balance, in time to secure the provisioning, could prove difficult.

As Pierre concluded his account of his day Simon produced his document with its offer of assistance to Pierre's proposed venture, given him by his new-found friend, the Consul for Genoa. Pierre did not attempt to conceal his joy at receiving this endorsement. After reading it aloud to all present, he held it up, in triumph, for all to see. Then, to the surprise of all, Pierre declared Simon his

Ambassador to Genoa. Simon would work closely with Signor Baggio to represent their interests and hopefully win the support of Genoa, to their cause. This would leave Pierre free to pursue other pressing responsibilities. However, if Signor Baggio proved truly committed to the undertaking, it might be possible to pass the responsibility of Genoa entirely to him, leaving Simon to concentrate on gaining the support of Venice, which they assumed, being a great sea-faring state, would readily agree to take a major role in such a marine activity.

Pierre shared with Simon his apprehensions about meeting with his older brother, Philip. Tensions had built over the years between the two brothers who were so dissimilar in their interests and ambitions. Although Pierre had happy memories of the first fifteen years of their lives, their relationship had held little emotional warmth. The pattern of their lives had pulled them apart and Pierre had little idea how Philip felt at that time and what his reaction would be. In that present situation it was he, Pierre who had the support of the Pope and his plans provided a common interest with his brother. It would offer Philip an alternative to the one chosen by his chief adversary, Frederic Barbarossa, self-styled Ruler of Christendom.

Philip's status, however, was enhanced by his own favour with the Pope and his renowned friendship with Richard Coeur de Lion. Their friendship went back to childhood and Philip hoped that it would soon be further strengthened by the planned marriage between Richard and his sister, Alice. This would produce a military alliance superior to any in the Christian world. Pierre was hoping for a warm welcome from Philip, when he offered his brother his allegiance and brought him a plan that would greatly further Philip's ambitions.

If Simon's persuasive skills were successful in gaining the commitment of Genoa and Venice, then Philip's support for Pierre's plan would guarantee Richard's co-operation and this in turn would ensure the success of the whole project. Taking advantage of Pierre's present relaxed state, Simon suggested that his fellow traveller, the Padre, should accompany him on his planned assignments, for the presence of a devout Christian would be most natural in negotiations that involved religious matters. Pierre agreed readily and immediately ordered that Father Dominic be instated as the religious leader of the vessel and Simon's companion in his future travels. In return for this trust, he gave Pierre unreserved assurance of his allegiance to him, the company and the cause. The decision made, a messenger was despatched, from a representative of His Holiness the Pope, to the Consul of Genoa, requesting a meeting to discuss a matter of religious and commercial importance to the city of Genoa.

The next day they arrived at the Consul's house just before noon as invited, and they were shown to a very stately reception hall, having left their escorting party in the inner courtyard. The Signor greeted Simon more like an old family friend than a new acquaintance and warmly welcomed Pierre and the Padre. When Pierre thanked his host for his speedy invitation, Signor Baggio explained that he had anticipated the request after his conversation with Simon. After the short formal introductions he took them through to the rear garden where lunch was prepared.

Their host then extended his invitation by informing them that the cook had already received instructions for the evening meal, when they were to be joined by a group of powerful and influential guests that the Signor had invited to dinner. They were also assured that rooms had been made ready for their overnight stay. As they entered the garden they were served wine in decorative glasses, filled from a beautiful marble carafe, held protectively close to the bosom of the cook's pretty daughter, who looked most eager to be of service. Pierre appreciatively took the offered goblet filled with dark cherry red wine, and after a first sip he nodded his approval towards his host and then the server. The attention of the cook's daughter did not swerve from Simon and her disappointment when he declined the wine was very obvious to all. Pierre wisely broke the tension between the two by commenting to Simon that the wine was excellent and well worth a try, expressing astonishment that such an excellent wine could be found outside of France. Simon, noticing the inquisitive atmosphere he had created, decided to accept the offered wine, to the approval of everyone and clearly the girl's delight and pleasure.

Leaving the remaining contents of the marble carafe on the low table, the servants departed. The company then turned their attention to Simon, but he averted his gaze and inquired of the Signor if his guest list for the evening included the Consul of Venice. Simon's unquestionable insight impressed his host as well as his friend Pierre, who was momentarily speechless. The Signor confirmed that the list of dignitaries invited included all those that he had deemed to be possibly interested participants in the business at hand. While all but the Padre were engrossed in conversation, Simon withdrew to a quiet corner to sample his first-ever alcoholic drink. As he allowed his tongue to investigate the taste, he was pleasantly surprised that, with little effort, he could convert it to its original state- a very palatable grape juice. While outwardly concentrating on this task he did not neglect to follow the conversations of those nearby.

As Simon had anticipated, the Padre, having been removed from his custodial surroundings on board, then finding himself in such esteemed company and unaccustomed surroundings, was quite overwhelmed. He was well aware that Simon had played a significant part in his changed condition. Simon found that engaging the Padre in conversation served a double purpose. It was a means of avoiding unnecessary small talk and also gave him the opportunity to put the Padre at his ease and begin the process of preparing him to be his major confidante. Simon stayed close to the Padre whilst taking note of the reactions of the other guests in relation to the night's agenda. He was conscious that Pierre had been striving to prove himself. He had found in his experience that this was not unusual in people who had no specific ambition or purpose and found themselves drifting aimlessly on the tide of life. Simon believed that Pierre had been in that state in the past. This, most certainly did not apply to their host that night. Signor Baggio was undoubtedly born to the position he held. His family ties to the city of Genoa and everything the Maritime Republic stood for, went back many generations and appeared set to continue well into the future. In comparison, the Venetian Consul appeared an exact mirror image. Outwardly, the two cities appeared in constant competition with obvious conflicts of interest. However, in the political and social arenas, both cities showed a front of great courtesy and sociability. The two states, whatever their differences, would always avoid military conflict as this would be costly to both sides and the main priority of both states was the accumulation of wealth. They had been trading competitors for generations and while they had never been partners, they had developed a system of co-existence, where they traded equally without infringing each other's markets. This was possible due to the vast trading capacity across the Mediterranean Sea.

The ancient Phoenicians had been the first sea-farers to exploit this potential and had maintained their supremacy until Genoa and Venice had followed the same path with unquestionable success. They now felt their position was being challenged. Spain's more recent aspiration to become a sea power was considered a threat to both and they also feared the Seljuk Turks who, although no challenge at sea, may have adversely affected their trade by producing certain restrictions on land trade routes that supplied the two sea ports.

On the night of the dinner, however, the guests had vital decisions to make. Certain factors were already unavoidable. The Third Crusade was already deemed necessary and preparations, the accumulation of manpower, collection of provisions, and the logistics of transport to harbours were already in hand. The opportunities for profit were limitless and, as Islamic sea power was virtually non-existent, there was minimal risk to vessels and crews. The success of this venture would secure the freedom of the trade routes for the foreseeable future by possibly eliminating the influence of the Turks of Byzantium, who held the canton Galata in Constantinople, and controlled the Genoese silk route.

The plan had all the guests completely focussed, but Simon suspected that each was busy calculating his own benefit. He guessed that only he and the Padre had no clear expectation of personal gain. He realised that this was about to be another in-depth learning experience for him. The Padre, deeply aware of the overwhelming debt he owed to his Islamic friend, was prepared to commit himself totally to the loyalty and companionship of Simon. Watching his friend move in such esteemed company, he could not fail to be impressed by his companion's bearing and the respect in which he was held. Looking around he concluded that in his position as a 'man of the cloth' his opinion would carry little weight and therefore there was wisdom in silence.

TEN

FATHER DOMINIC

Having decided that the Padre was to be his friend and companion, Simon sought to learn more of his background.

The Padre was Dominic. He was the middle son of farming family, solid and dependable. They were not very prosperous but had good, fertile land, not far from Lisbon. Dominic was a quiet, thoughtful boy interested in the world around him and particularly the community in which he lived. From an early age he had understood that the family farm land was not large enough to be divided between the brothers and so it would ultimately be inherited by his elder brother, as was the common practice at the time. When he was not needed on the family farm he would often offer his labour to other farms and vineyards, where he was always welcomed as he had a reputation as a good, reliable and willing worker. However, he was hardly a rarity in this as the country-side abounded with youngsters like Dominic, looking for gainful employment to help out the family budget. Whenever he could not find employment he would offer his services to the local priest and would assist him in the church and also in the spacious kitchen gardens. Although he was not paid in money, he was rewarded by tuition in reading and writing.

Dominic proved a ready student and this led to his being recommended for a position at the nearby Dominican Abbey. Before long the artistry of his hand-writing impressed the Abbot and he was asked to assist in the compilation of the Abbey's history. The Abbot had undertaken this task many years before, but as he aged his hand-writing had deteriorated and he was no longer satisfied with his own work. Many of the other monks had helped in the gathering of information by researching the archives, but they were all getting older and the Abbot was determined that his project must be completed in his lifetime.

The young Dominic was welcomed by all. Eventually his position as the Abbey scribe, his good health and relative youth were all high recommendations when he was assigned as religious leader to the expeditionary fleet organised by the King of Portugal. He was expected to assist the fleet navigator in preparing new charts of the territories they encountered in order to prepare a route for future Portuguese sailors to reach India and beyond to Japan, well clear of the interfering Turks, Genoese and Venetians.

In the opulent home of Signor Baggio he felt uncomfortable. The surroundings and distinguished company were unfamiliar to him. He would have preferred the confines of the rope store. It was a mystery to him how Simon, a young man from the orient, with a very different background, looked perfectly at ease with the company and their very intense conversations.

Simon gave no indication of the peculiar loneliness he was feeling in that company, that had been so carefully selected to suit his purpose, but he was comforted by feeling no sense of animosity towards him from anyone in the party. He could feel the warmth of friendship of Pierre, an almost paternal fondness from the Signor, a devoted loyalty from Dominic and only a slight reticence from the consul of Venice. However, in the case of the latter it was almost certainly more his reaction to the project than to Simon himself, to whom he showed a friendly approval. In spite of this Simon detected a certain innuendo in that gentleman's conversation that troubled him and he needed to consult his friends for guidance. He was confident that he could count on Pierre's co-operation, Signor Baggio's wisdom and sympathetic ear and Dominic's friendship and support, but they each had their own agenda and might find his particular position in the planned expedition difficult to comprehend. Although he had no doubt of Dominic's loyalty, he knew that the Padre still had some misgivings about Simon's true skills. In spite of this Simon remembered Musa's advice; that he should look for someone he could trust and then gradually shadow and mould him towards the supportive role he would take in the future. He had already decided that Dominic should be the one to fill that role.

Of one thing Simon was sure, that in spite of all the plans and organisation, the expedition against the Islamic world was not going to achieve all its aspirations. He felt that as he had been drawn into the conflict through no actions of his own, it could be his mission in life to serve humanity and his god by aiming to minimise the human anguish and loss of life that would inevitably result from the venture. He had no idea at that stage what his options might ultimately be. As far as that momentous evening was concerned all seemed to have gone smoothly, with the main complication of the day being the sampling of his very first alcoholic drink. He was still a little concerned about his difficulty in interpreting Signor Viyalli's reaction to the evening revelations, but surmised that the Consul had his own vision of the venture that would bring greater benefit to his own city, Venice.

Pierre proposed that Simon and Father Dominic should be dispatched, in haste, to Genoa and then on to Venice, carrying a copy of the Papal documents and the recommendations of that evening's group. They were to make clear that the committee formed that evening included Pierre and also the representatives of the two Maritime Republics. Both Consuls agreed to this without reservations and this closed the formal business of the night. All present raised their glasses in a jovial celebration toast to the success of the venture and the night ended in harmony and with the crucial proceedings launched.

Simon later admitted that that had been one of the most tiring and trying days of his life.

When he eventually retired to his bed, sleep arrived without invitation and kept him wrapped in its comfort well into the next morning.

Before he opened his eyes, he felt the presence of another person in his room. Feigning sleep he observed the servant girl standing by the window intently watching him. He gradually went through the normal ritual of awakening and gave the expected look of surprise when he acknowledged her in his room. He was also genuinely surprised to find that he had been sleeping in the same room, from which he had seen her watching him the previous day. She was staring at him with a dreamy look in her eyes but Simon pretended not to notice any implication in her gaze. Anxious not to give her encouragement, he slipped modestly from his bed, took a few deep breaths at the open window, splashed his face with the cool water from the basin the girl had brought and took the towel from her willing hands. After dressing suitably for the day ahead, Simon thanked the girl with a friendly smile and inquired as to the whereabouts of his host. She informed him that the Signor always woke by sunrise and took his breakfast at the table under the lilac tree, where he attended to the documents of the day.

Simon approached the Signor, wishing him a good morning, and was greeted cheerfully in return and shown to a chair next to his host. The Signor was clearly most anxious to hear from Simon his impressions of the previous night's business. After thanking his friend for his hospitality and for the valuable support he had given to Pierre's project, Simon went on to express his concern over Signor Viyalli's unspoken reservations.

Signor Baggio was pleasantly surprised by Simon's insight into the Venetian Consul's thoughts as he was of a similar opinion, but he understood that this was due to a lifetime involvement in deep-seated local politics of which Simon could not possibly be aware. The Signor proceeded to explain.

"There are practical and fundamental differences in the trade practises of the two Maritime Republics.

The trade in Genoa is mainly from China through secure land transport, normally by caravans to the Black Sea shores, then transferred to storage depositories at Galata, which is a Genoese protectorate on the outskirts of Constantinople, on the shores of the Golden Horn. These practices are subject to long-term agreements brought about by historical alliances between various trading partners. From these stores traders transport the goods to outlets throughout Europe. The recently proposed course of action would not endanger this practice.

On the other hand, Venice is dependent on their agreements with Saladin and others to secure their trade routes to India. The proposed venture would, without doubt endanger their agreements. And so, dear Simon, this information may help you to understand more clearly Signor Viyalli's hesitation in welcoming your anticipated mission."

Simon was impressed by his friend's clear analysis and calm acceptance of the facts and also by the efficient manner in which he had already prepared the papers for himself and Father Dominic to carry to the two city councils.

Simon was increasingly conscious of the great responsibility being placed on him and also aware that this almost certainly would place him in conflict with his own people. However, he determined to fulfil his obligations to all hopefully without destroying his personal integrity.

ELEVEN

NORTH TO GENOA

The sail along the west coast to Genoa was uneventful. Simon continued his regular communications with his parents at sunrise, to keep them informed of his activities.

At one point he considered contacting his old teacher, Musa but decided against it, as talking about his skills may appear like boasting, for which he had no time. Instead he concentrated on developing a deeper relationship of trust and understanding with his friend Father Dominic. This resulted in his confessing to the Padre, after being assured of the latter's total discretion, that he had been delegated to approach powerful people in Genoa, to negotiate their participation in a vastly important political undertaking. He confided that he was only a temporary messenger and held no permanent position of power. He did share his apprehension that there might be times when he would need the support and even the protection of a trusted friend, and he asked Dominic if he was prepared to fulfil that role.

The poor Padre nearly fainted with surprise at the

honour that was being paid him, as this assignment was far beyond the wildest expectations of a cleric of his humble standing. Again, he realised the depth of gratitude he owed to this young man who had brought him to the notice of higher authorities. Simon then cautioned Dominic to be discreet over their relationship and mission as jealousy and prejudice may put them in danger.

The reputation of Signor Baggio and his family extended far beyond a signature on the letter that Simon held. The near reverence in which the Signor was held made a significant difference to the status of Simon and Dominic, both on board the vessel and most certainly when they finally reached the city of Genoa.

The two companions were housed with one of the senior merchant families in very favourable lodgings and in due course were escorted to the High Consul Chamber to present their credentials. They were received by the President of the Consulate, the Bishop of Genoa, who ruled under his overlord, the Holy Roman Emperor. Simon presented the statements they were carrying on behalf of the Holy Roman See and also the correspondence from the Consul of Genoa and the Committee who had assigned him his task.

The impressive building and the magnificence of the Chamber reflected the vast opulence of the Consulate and the status of the Consuls. In the galleries around the Chamber sat representatives of all the great merchant houses of Genoa. Simon noticed that some families had more than one representative present and as these families appeared to have their own defined areas he assumed that it was an indication of the importance of the family.

When the reading of the documents was completed there was a slight pause in proceedings, which provided Simon with an opportunity to look around and observe the representatives more closely.

Almost immediately he found himself being introduced as the messenger who had carried the documents from the Holy See and the bearer of the recommendations from their Consul in Rome. It had not gone unnoticed that the committee in Rome had included both the Venetian Consul and the Frankish representative. It was also mentioned in the introduction that he was a navigator on a vessel, despatched by the King of Portugal, to chart a new passage to India and China.

Both Simon and Dominic were taken aback by the alarm the last statement had caused among the Assembly. Everyone was aware that the discovery of a new passage to these territories, which would not be under their direct control, would threaten the monopolies they had enjoyed for many years. Portugal had never been in competition with Genoa in the past, but they had always respected the country as a sea-faring nation with potential. If Portugal could by-pass the turbulent political intrigues of Byzantine Constantinople, the banditry on the roads through Asia, and also avoid any encounters with Venice, (a permanent thorn to Genoa and a natural suspect in any act of piracy whenever a Genoese vessel failed to reach its destined harbour), then Portugal could prove to be a dependable provider at a more economic rate than Genoa and so would pose a great threat to their city's life force.

Simon immediately realised that he now faced possibly his greatest challenge to date. His exposé of the plan had to be at the same time, clear, simple and concise, humble and prudent and yet it must appear appealing to his audience and allay their fears.

He was aware that most of those in the hall were merchants, but there were also a few who had pretensions to royalty. Each one represented immense wealth, either accrued or inherited and all shared a common goal- to hold on to what they had and increase it whenever possible. Some were directly involved in maritime transport and owners of ships, while others were merchants and traders.

The questions addressed to Simon all reflected the concerns of dedicated people who had knowledge and experience and were keen to understand the full effect the proposed quest would have on their livelihood and territory and how it was that Portugal, a country not renowned for its sea-faring history was the originator of this venture.

Simon stood and started tentatively to explain the difficulties encountered by Portugal, a Christian country, which had ventured on to the sea out of necessity, due to shortage of sufficient land to sustain its population. Fishing had been a major industry, but as the population grew, trading expanded beyond their country's boundaries, first to neighbouring countries and then further afield. Because of its geographical position this required Portugal to take to the sea and so its vessels had entered the Mediterranean, the trading centre of the western world. He explained that it was not the need for adventure nor the desire for domination, but the hope of finding new trading opportunities that drove them into such a perilous venture. And so he attempted to reassure them that Portugal was not wishing to compete against Genoa and Venice but merely trying to broaden its trading horizons for the benefit of all traders. He went on:

"Are we not all aware that trade can only get better by expansion and healthy competition? As for Portugal, there has been no increase in trade so far, but there has been the acquisition and accumulation of valuable information. The expedition to the Far East in search of new routes showed without doubt that many of the charts and maps in regular use are quite inaccurate. The Ocean, for example, is much greater than was previously believed, and this alone calls into question many previous perceptions. We are no closer to a trading post, or the expectation of one in the near future. Our expeditionary fleet travelled much further than we had anticipated, but we still have no idea of the full potential of these territories."

There were rows of comfortable seats positioned under magnificently decorated and colourful banners belonging to the various trading houses. These seats were occupied by men, a number of whom were or had been sea captains of many years' experience. They would certainly be in a position to appreciate the situation that Simon was describing.

As he scanned the galleries to assess the reaction to his speech his attention was caught by a sad young man seated in the centre gallery. Simon's trained instinct told him that the fellow had good reason to be troubled.

TWELVE

THE TALE OF CAPTAIN DORIA

In an instant Simon's mind was party to the young man's story. Apparently he had returned home after a long journey from his distant trading post in Galata, on the shores of the Golden Horn. He carried with him many presents for his beloved young wife. Anxious to greet his wife after his long absence, he did not notice his servants' looks of alarm at his unexpected arrival. He rushed, without hesitation, straight to his private rooms. Flinging open the door he was devastated to find his beautiful wife asleep, naked on their bed with her arm draped across the body of a young servant who lay nestled against her body. Shaking with rage he grabbed the servant and flung him unceremoniously through the open window into the courtyard below. The commotion had woken his wife and as he moved from the window she turned to him with such a beautiful smile that in spite of his rage his heart melted. He understood well the extreme behaviour that intense loneliness could cause.

As he looked at her he remembered all the other

beautiful things in his life that he loved; the glorious red sunsets over the Sea of Marmaris, that he had watched so often from the terrace of his villa on the Princes Island of Cybele; walking through the island's pine forests down to the shoreline and his anger was further abated and his heart warmed. He was home now and it would not happen again.

He had been born into a wealthy family and had always been content with his own company, possibly due in part, to being the only boy in a family of girls. His three sisters were excellent company for each other, though always a problem for their mother and engaged most of her time. Feeling that he had to compete so fiercely for his mother's attention made him a little jealous and left him resentful of women generally. His father was often away at sea for long periods, but when the boy was fifteen years old, his father asked if he would like to accompany him on his next voyage. Just like Simon had been, he was ecstatic at the prospect.

It was at sea that he found his own individuality and his true vocation. He recognised instantly that it was what he wanted. The life was disciplined and every action had a purpose. In the early years he was following his captain's orders, and later when he was captain, had the responsibility of issuing them.

In his personal life he had been guided by his family to marry into a neighbouring family, but one much older, wealthier and more powerful than his. It was a dynastic family that needed an heir. The marriage was arranged by the consent of all and was a very extravagant and public affair. He was young and energetic and had proved himself dependable, able and ambitious, while she was the most beautiful girl he had ever seen. His future looked bright, indeed. Unfortunately their lavish honeymoon was to last too short a time, as he had important business in Batumi, in Georgia. He had to receive merchandise that was due to arrive by caravan from the Far East. If he failed to collect it, there would be an opportunity for other merchants to bribe the purchase of the goods. While his departure was expected, his bride was distressed to lose the warm companionship she had so enjoyed for such a short time, as he would be away for many months.

It was while he was in Batumi that the news reached him that his wife was pregnant. Both families had been overjoyed and had celebrated the joyful news in the Captain's absence.

When the welcome news reached the delighted father he lost all sense of reason and celebrated in a most unseemly manner. Later, he could only partially recall the events, due to a heavy, over-indulgence of wine, drunk in the private company of two Greek beauties, twin sisters, with whom he had enjoyed a long-standing relationship. He convinced himself that he was only behaving as rich and powerful men do in such circumstances and that it was to be expected. Never did he question whether his new bride would agree to such excesses.

Remembering his own errant behaviour and feeling some responsibility for her loneliness, he warmed to her smile, knowing that he could never raise an eyebrow let alone a hand in anger against her. He also knew that even had he been tempted, it would have been a final act as her family, the Spinolas, were not known for their tolerance or forgiveness. And so the entire unhappy episode had been put behind them and the young couple had proceeded with their lives.

However, whisper of the unfortunate event must have travelled beyond the walls of the family households- (perhaps some indiscreet servant had been disloyal) for, as Captain Doria stood up to address the Consulate, everyone fell silent and the atmosphere vibrated with anticipation. Almost unintelligible with embarrassment, but driven on by his sense of public duty, the captain offered his recently re-fitted flag ship to accommodate not only members of his own family but also any Royal passengers that might participate in the venture. He added modestly that he was honoured to be in a position to make such an offer. This was greeted with great acclaim and it appeared that any censure there may have been had been dispelled.

There followed further pledges of solidarity. It was then proposed that 65% of the maritime vessels bearing the standards of the city of Genoa be made available for the venture and should be placed under the command of Captain Doria, who was immediately promoted to the rank of Admiral.

In recognition of his services to the trade of Genoa, Simon was granted the honour of Freeman of the City and given the rank of Captain of the Consular Guard. That day's events were remembered for many years to come. The unknown youth who had been so successful in winning over even the most hardened sceptic became legendary.

The Bishop and the Consuls declared two days of holiday and the bells of the city rang out to make this known to all the citizens. The aged father of Signor Baggio, who had an honoured position in the Consulate invited all present to an evening of celebration at his family estate. It turned out to be a very splendid occasion with so many dignitaries mingling in an atmosphere of relaxed harmony. The most noticeable amongst the guests was Lady Doria, looking serene and beautiful and radiating contentment since she and her Admiral husband had put their past troubles behind them. Together they were the toast of the party.

Simon and the Padre enjoyed the scene, observing from a distance and taking little part in the conversation. Partway through the evening they were introduced to Lady and Admiral Doria. Simon was immediately attracted to the young couple and felt a strong bond of friendship forming with them.

The Elders of the Consulate had decided that Simon and his entourage had earned their protection and should be granted safe passage on their way to Venice. An armed escort in the charge of one of the Sergeant at Arms of the Council and the Pope's Seal would accompany them on their journey.

The next morning Simon was escorted to the guards' officer quarters to be kitted out with the uniform appropriate to his new rank. Out of sentiment and perhaps a little homesickness, he still concealed his beloved mother's jacket beneath his outer garments.

He was then invited to choose weapons from the armoury. He found a dagger of good quality. He looked for a sword, but found them mostly over decorated and impractical. He finally spotted one that he recognised as folded steel. While it was generally of a good length and weight, he had matured physically over the months at sea, and the sword needed some adjustment to handle perfectly. On enquiring for a blacksmith he was directed to a forge in the barrack's courtyard. The farrier proved most helpful and sent his assistant off to the local butcher to acquire the deer antlers and shin bones that Simon requested. The apprentice returned laying a selection of bones on the floor from which Simon made his choice. Meanwhile the blacksmith had removed the hilt and placed the blade in the furnace. At red heat, Simon carefully manipulated the blade giving it a slight curve at the one end and then honed the double edge to a lethal sharpness. While the metal was again re-heated, Simon took a hammer and smashed his selected bones on an anvil until they were each a fine powder. When he was satisfied, he removed the sword from the heat and buried it in the powdered horn. He left it there for a long time before removing it and burnishing the blade to a mirror finish. He repeated the process with the second powder before cooling it in liquid lard. He was now confident that no other sword could match his for strength, and that if he ever found himself in combat, his sword would never fail him.

He was now ready to take his leave of the city that had given him so warm a welcome. He was happy to know that at least some of the inhabitants, he was destined to meet again.

THIRTEEN

EAST TOWARDS VENICE

A s Simon and his companions left Genoa on their journey towards the Maritime Republic of Venice, he realised again how limited his life experience had been. Even approaching the harbour of Genoa on their arrival, he had been impressed by the height of the surrounding mountains that formed a backdrop to the city. His journey took him directly into the pine-forested hills that rose behind the town and as he had spent his youth on the lowland plains of Mesopotamia, he found the vista awe-inspiring. He had previously believed that such altitudes could only be achieved by birds or clouds. Simon had always been gifted with a good sense of direction. Even as a child he had watched the sun rise through one window in the morning and drop below the horizon through another in the evening. This innate sense, enhanced by his education, had guided him through deserts and across oceans, but he found that on the narrow animal tracks on the steep slopes of a densely wooded mountain the skill deserted him completely. Consequently he was very glad of his companions' familiarity with the terrain. He was also grateful for their advice on his clothing, for within three days of leaving Genoa they found the temperature dropped dramatically and he was glad of the cumbersome but warm clothing that, in his innocence, he had believed to be unnecessary. The one person who did not object to the drop in temperature was the Padre, whose thick woollen cloak, so uncomfortable in the heat, stood him in good stead.

They maintained as steady an ascent as possible, but the continuous incline was unavoidable and every increase in altitude contributed to Simon's discomfort and he used all his earlier training to control his breathing.

In all the villages they passed through they encountered a warm welcome. At times they were greeted with such enthusiasm that Simon felt embarrassed. They were invited to dine and rest in the wealthiest of households, if the local priest had not already laid claim to their company.

Simon concentrated all his skills on mentally and physically adapting to the unaccustomed temperature and altitude, and he soon found he could adopt a more positive response to his changed surroundings.

The horses, transporting their heavy loads, also suffered badly from the cold and the rarefied air.

On the seventh day of their journey they reached the limit of Genoa's jurisdiction and they agreed that they would approach the Venetian territories without their full party. Simon did not wish to appear aggressive or over defensive and so draw unwelcome attention. Half the company, along with the ailing horses, were left in the care of the monks at the last monastery, where they would await the return of the ambassadorial party and its diminished escort.

It was on the third night after the party had split and the reduced group had been travelling through forest and rocks with very little fertile soil to provide sustenance, when Simon offered to stand the midnight watch, with the Padre as companion. They were in a small clearing situated on a high mountain ledge overlooking a valley, with a crystal-clear lake that reflected a perfect mirror image of distant, snow-capped peaks. The sight of the snow sent shivers along Simon's spine. He sat propped against a massive, ancient pine tree as he gazed, mesmerized, into the eternal, unfathomable depths of the water. He pressed his heels into the protruding rock in front of him and watched the last light of the day fade, leaving him in darkness, alone with his own deep thoughts.

He became conscious that someone or something was speaking to him. Although his ears did not register any sound the message was clear. *"If you continue to push like you are, you may end up within me, young being."*

Simon looked around him for an explanation. He glanced across at the Padre who was seated close by, lost in his own thoughts and completely unaware of Simon's predicament.

"If you relax and lean against me gently as you did before I may let you into my body."

Remembering his earlier experiences with the dolphins and birds he came to the conclusion that he was receiving a message from the spirit of the tree. He relaxed all his physical and mental tension, gently eased his body against the great tree and closed his eyes. The first sensation he felt was like countless ants rushing through him toward the top of the tree. He realised that what he was experiencing was the sap being drawn up from the roots through a maze of arteries into the branches and the leaves. Gradually he lost his identity in the tree and became part of its essence. He moved with the sap, he was the roots, the trunk, the leaves. His first reaction was the apprehension of an intruder but he immediately understood that he was, in fact, accepted by the tree.

"How long have you been here?" Simon asked, and he was not surprised by the answer he received.

"I have been here since ancient times and now many of the forests from the sunrise to the sunset, as well as to the north, are my offspring or the descendants of my offspring. Sometimes we play together to create storms, affecting weather to our design and causing disturbances out to sea, far to the south, east or west. We are in constant communication and now my children tell me there is a company of men approaching from the east who intend you harm. Do you wish to return to your friends and warn them of this?"

Simon thanked the Great Tree for allowing him an amazing experience and gradually eased his spirit back into his body. Fortunately, the Padre had heard the advancing party in the distance and had alerted the companions before disturbing Simon, whom he believed to be in a deep sleep.

The escort were all well-trained guards who did not require instruction from a leader and were instantly ready to face a potential foe.

Quite suddenly they were surrounded. Simon gripped his sword that lay beside him and flicked it from its scabbard. He raised himself just in time to parry a short sword lunge from one of the attackers. Realising that he was unbalanced and ill-prepared for a second blow, he held his breath in anticipation of feeling pain. The darkness was intense and he could not see his adversary. Not feeling the effect of an immediate blow, he moved sideways and encouraged his sword towards the line of the previous attack. With a short, sharp movement he sliced deeply at his adversary's neck and felt the man fall at his feet. At each attack Simon's responses were instinctive and economic. His movement was disciplined, almost choreographed. On later reflection it reminded him of the Whirling Dervishes, devout followers of Sufi performing their ritual dance of twirling, perpetual motion, in which they reach a level of contemplation between two dimensions, two time channels, past and future. This was believed to give them a state of invincibility that protected them from harm even from the sword. Anxious to protect his companions and himself but also to preserve precious life, he aimed at arms and legs to render his assailants harmless but not endanger their lives. He moved swiftly among his opponents, slipping lightly over roots and rocks, maintaining the balance of a dancer. Remembering his father's teaching that a thrust always required a withdrawal, he used only the cutting tip of his sword to damage and maim, then moved on the next adversary without delay.

It soon became obvious that Simon was the main target of the attack. This realisation spurred him on with renewed vigour, as his enemies came on to him. In a short time the defenders had the advantage and the last three uninjured attackers were surrounded and the Sergeant at

Arms offered to spare their lives if they surrendered their weapons.

It was then that Simon looked around him for the Padre and found him seated at the base of the Great Pine tree. He realised immediately that his friend was in great discomfort and hurried to his side. Dominic's vision was glazed and he was unconscious. Alarmed by his friend's dire condition, Simon reached out to test for a pulse both at the heart and in the side of the neck. Satisfied that his friend was alive, he lifted the heavy woollen habit and discovered a deep sword wound just below the heart. Placing his hand on the wound he gently probed to the deepest point of the sword's penetration. Without conscious thought, he drew on his own psychic energy to start repairing the damaged tissue. It felt like an eternity, even to those around him, and for Simon time stood still. Eventually he leaned his head against the tree trunk for a moment's respite, then stood and walked towards a broad-leaved plant. Returning to the patient with two leaves, he carefully removed the transparent layer from within the leaves and placed it on the wound, which was no longer bleeding, and used the rest of the leaves for padding around the wound. He removed his shirt and folded it carefully using the cleanest part as a bandage. With the assistance of the sergeant he laid the Padre in a more comfortable position wrapping him warmly in his habit and cloak.

Simon then pressed both his hands flat on the ground, drawing deeply on the earth's natural energy to replenish that which was spent from his body due to his recent exertions. When he felt himself refreshed he eased himself to a standing position.

It was as though this was the signal for time, which had been paused, to re-start. On seeing Simon stand, one of the three prisoners lunged at another, with the obvious intention of assassinating him. The Sergeant at Arms deflected the blow and then hit the assailant hard over the head with the pummel of his sword knocking him to the ground. His fellow guards soon overpowered the other two and tied all three securely.

They then turned their attention to the morbid task of disposing of the dead. They found an area of soft ground and set to work to dig a pit, large enough for a mass burial.

Simon, appreciating the calm expertise of the sergeant, asked him to take the place of the injured Padre and perform the necessary Christian ceremony. And so, when all items of value had been removed from the bodies, in accordance with normal procedures, the dead were laid to rest. When the proceedings were completed, Simon, unused to deadly combat, was physically and emotionally exhausted. He was having a problem focussing on the proceedings around him. The Genoese guards, seeing his condition, had sympathy realising that they had been hardened to the experience by their training, which Simon had not. They had admired the manner in which Simon had handled himself, not only in the fighting, but also in the way he had tended to the Padre's injury, although they did not expect the priest to survive. They respected Simon's predicament and withdrew to a distance and settled down for a well-deserved rest. Simon slowly eased Dominic on to a bed of soft undergrowth and tucked more around him to keep him snug. Happy that his friend was resting comfortably he walked over to the rest of the party and enquired after their well-being. Surprisingly, they had suffered only minor casualties which they had attended to themselves. Simon thanked them all for their bravery and commitment and then inquired of the Sergeant at Arms, his assessment of the attackers and their motives. The Sergeant said that he and his men had been discussing the question among themselves and were convinced that the assailants were too well-trained and disciplined to be simply bandits. They had sought out Simon as a target and so had been carefully briefed. The foiled attempt at self-destruction was indicative of a well-planned and well-paid operation, with the threat of serious retaliation against themselves or their families in the case of failure or captivity by their target. While they were fierce fighting men it was believed they would not hold out against skilled interrogators. As the assessment was in line with his own thinking Simon indicated to the sergeant to follow him. He walked over to the captives and cut their restricting bonds, telling them: "I am of the opinion that you were assigned to prevent this company reaching its destination. We have no intention of harming you and for that reason we have decided not to press on to Venice. In that sense you may feel that you have accomplished your undertaking. Unfortunately, if you return to Venice you will have to find an explanation for the events which have taken place, but my suspicion is that your appearance may prove to be an undesirable problem for your city rulers. So I am allowing you until sunrise to decide whether you take your chance on a return to Venice, become a loyal part of my group, or settle on some other option."

Then, addressing all present, he recommended them to get a good night's sleep and prepare for the day ahead.

Before leaving, the Sergeant glanced questioningly again towards the Padre but did not speak. Simon knew that the men had observed his healing actions and had wondered about it. Feeling he owed the Sergeant some explanation, he said,

"I fear I am not as skilled in healing as I appeared, but doing nothing in such circumstances is not in my nature. As for our Padre, I believe that an undisturbed period of rest may help the natural healing processes of his body and eventually bring him back to full consciousness. With God's help, in a day or two we may again enjoy our friend's company and on that day we shall start our return journey to Genoa, for I now believe that our presence in Venice will not be beneficial to either our cause or our health".

The Sergeant happily agreed with Simon's decision and on wishing each other a good night they both retired to rest. As Simon's mind drifted at the fringe of sleep, he wondered if trees could show animosity to each other. He would never be sure whether it was in his dream or from the spirit of the Great Rock Pine, that he heard the message,

"This was not the first time we have witnessed men maltreat each other. Being alive among our own kind will frequently present us with situations that we need to deal with. Handling these situations well and being able to move on successfully for the good of all, may be a real purpose for our existence. When you are finally ready to leave this spot it will not be the parting of our friendship for you will always be able to contact me through your Mind's Eye. At *times I can communicate with the birds that are born in my branches, but when they fly away, I usually lose contact with them. However, you are my first human contact and our bond is very strong. I believe we shall be able to communicate for a very long time even from great distances."*

Early the next day the three former prisoners approached Simon and the sergeant, who were organising a stretcher for the Padre. They knelt humbly in front of them and swore an oath of loyalty to hold for the rest of their lives. They had agreed with Simon's assessment and knew they would be at grave risk if they returned to Venice. They apologised for the injury to the Padre, saying they would never have imagined anyone putting his body as a shield to protect a friend, but as they had also watched Simon tending his friend's wound they had realised the strength of a bond that could exist between true friends. Their declaration confirmed what Simon had suspected about the action of his friend and he understood clearly then, that he possibly owed his life to Dominic's self-less act.

Two days later the Padre was fully conscious and able to take a little water and moist biscuits. His full recovery soon followed. He was amazed to find no trace of the wound existed and he confided the fact to Simon. He was barely surprised when Simon told him that as it was the first time he had tried to heal someone, perhaps they should keep it to themselves.

And so with the Padre fit to travel and bonds of friendship formed, that would ensure life-long companionship and loyalty to Simon, the group turned west to make the return journey to Genoa.

Their slow progress inadvertently enabled a message

from Venice to reach Genoa ahead of them. In spite of the attack on the party, that had obviously been politically motivated, the Venetian Consulate was officially offering full co-operation in all aspects of the planned venture. This news caused Simon to strictly censure the information about the attack and the reason for their return, believing that the fewer people that knew the better. He felt, in this case, confidentiality was the essence of diplomacy.

On their arrival in Genoa, Simon was not surprised to hear that a very considerable armada had assembled in various ports and harbours along the coasts of southern Europe but few were flying the Venetian standard.

A very large and disorganised movement of Royalty and Nobles with their accompanying entourage, knights, clerics and men at arms was travelling south to the French, Spanish and Italian port cities. This movement was followed by the transport of stores, live animals, soldiers and their supporting engineers as well as a large number of the usual adventurers which formed a never-ending procession across Europe.

Simon, the Padre and his faithful companions soon found themselves on board the newly converted and re-named Bella Doria, where Simon took up his appointed post of Chief Navigator to the entire Mission.

Unable to accompany her husband since she had so recently given birth to her child, Lady Doria, was seen on the quayside holding her baby son, wishing her husband, the Admiral, a fond farewell and waving the ship off as the sailors upped anchors and set sail towards Marseilles and the start of the campaign.

This first part of their voyage was short and on arrival

at Marseilles, Simon met with the other leaders of the flotilla and shared with them his routes and proposed schedules.

They observed many ships in the harbour already loaded with cargo and passengers and making ready to sail, but the Admiral informed Simon that they would be preparing the Bella Doria for the arrival of a very important passenger and his party. The waiting time would be spent cleaning and polishing every inch of the ship.

It was on the third day of waiting that, no less a person than King Philip Augustus of the Franks arrived with his immediate family and attendants, filling the Bella Doria to the brim and rafters. Simon had not witnessed the arrival of the passengers as he was occupied preparing charts for the voyage and making draft copies for the Captains of the other ships. It was only later that Simon learnt the identity of their Royal passenger and that Philip had asked for a meeting to be arranged with King William the 11 of Sicily.

FOURTEEN

SIR SIMON OF SALAMIS

A fair wind eased their passage south. Simon's quarters were located on the aft deck, and it was the most spacious cabin he had ever enjoyed. He had a hammock to sleep in and a locker for his meagre possessions. He found it, altogether, very satisfactory.

It was the first night out of harbour when he went on deck to gather star references. He almost walked into a gathering of ladies, who happened to be admiring the bright and vibrant star-studded night sky, visible from horizon to horizon. A number of the stars even appeared to be communicating with each other as they shimmered and winked. Unwilling to disturb the star-gazers, Simon's first instinct was to step back into his cabin but he was already too far to not be noticed, so he moved forward slowly avoiding their attention. He kept a respectful distance while he took his measurements and then discreetly moved back towards his cabin. He noticed that the watch and the helms-man were similarly minding their posts without being visible to the ladies.

It was a soft but authoritative voice that brought his progress to a halt.

"Young man!"

He slowly turned to the direction of the voice and bowed politely, while shyly keeping his eyes firmly fixed on the decking beneath him.

"Do approach," was the next command, which Simon obeyed by halving the distance between the two of them at an unhurried pace, stopping at what he judged to be a respectful distance.

"Will you give us your name and explain your task?"

Simon noticed a slender diadem hanging from the neck of his questioner.

"My name is Simon, Your Royal Highness, and I hold the post of navigator on this ship. I was observing the position of that particularly bright star which is called Polaris, and calculating its distance from the horizon. This will help me in following our navigational charts."

"You are a very youthful navigator, Master Simon, but we trust in your ability to guide us safely to our destination. We ladies have little knowledge of such matters and we would be pleased if you could enlighten us."

Simon attempted to explain that his knowledge had been accumulated through the ages from very early times. It started when man first began to travel and needed signs to follow, in order to retrace his steps. He would look to the stars for guidance. It was accepted that several of the stars, for reasons not yet understood, maintained a very stable position, which could be used for determining locations on earth. He daringly went on to propound his theory, based of the work of Aristarchus the Greek, that everything observed in the night sky, apart from the moon, was far greater in dimension than the earth. It was also believed that the stars resembled the sun and were in fact centres of other celestial systems as the sun was the centre of the earth's orbit.

At the moment when he feared he was getting too involved and veering too far from accepted principle, and so was looking for a means of escape, he was rescued by the appearance of the King, accompanied by the Admiral. They walked out on to the balcony that roofed the top of the mid castle, and attracted the attention of the ladies giving Simon the welcome opportunity to pay his respects and slip back to his cabin.

(The balcony where the King stood was surrounded by a protective and decorative balustrade and formed part of the extension that the Admiral had added to accommodate his family, and now housed the royal party. It was a unique feature never seen on a merchant vessel previously. The whole galley was extended by the length of the structure which allowed a third mast to be added. The effect of the modification on the appearance and comfort of the ship was incomparable. The extended hull even improved sea-worthiness, steering and speed of the vessel, to a noticeable degree.)

Simon had made every effort to avoid contact with their royal passengers, partly because he felt uncomfortable in such noble presence, but also because he spent most of his time preparing charts.

One afternoon he was studying charts that he had prepared, with a view to modifying them, when a crew member appeared informing him that he was requested to present himself before the King without delay. Simon left his work and was escorted to the King immediately.

He found the King already seated, in the company of the Admiral. They appeared to be enjoying a very dark red wine that they held in transparent decorative goblets. The King indicated to the Admiral to serve Simon but Simon declined the offer of wine, explaining that he was working on charts and he needed a clear head.

The King opened the interview with the astounding words,

"We have heard a great deal about you from many sources, young Simon, and all of it to your credit."

It soon became obvious that the King had heard of the exploits on the road to Venice, in spite of Simon's discretion. He was clearly impressed by Simon's alleged fighting ability and asked how he had acquired such excellent skills. Apparently, the King had asked the same question of Simon's loyal friend, the Padre, who had been unable to enlighten him. Simon informed the King that he owed most of his knowledge and skill to his parents. He explained that his father was a much travelled merchant sailor and accomplished captain and navigator, with wide knowledge and experience, which he had passed on to his son. From the loving-care of his mother he had developed a sense of self-worth and a deep sense of responsibility towards others. Although, as a youth, he had a tutor in the combative and military arts he had never had to use those skills until the unfortunate encounter that had been brought to the King's attention. He suggested that it must have been a strong desire for survival and a large degree of fortune that assisted them all to overcome that particular danger.

The King declared that Simon was, perhaps, being too

modest. But then quite suddenly he changed the subject and challenged Simon over his conversation with the ladies, some of which he had obviously overheard.

"But what about your telling the ladies that the stars are larger than the earth, when all the Church's teaching proclaims that the earth is the centre of the Universe?" Simon realised that he had to step carefully not to be accused of heresy. He explained that while he was prepared to accept all the teachings of Christ without question, he always reserved his judgement on other matters until he had fully investigated the circumstances. There were a number of theories related to the topic he had been discussing with the ladies. While the one accepted at that time had been proposed by Aristotle, and suggested that the earth was the centre of the Universe, he was inclined to favour the opposing view of Aristarchus that propounded that it was, in fact, the sun that was the centre and the earth and other planets revolved around it. While his own observations led him to that belief, he accepted that there was little proof or certainty either way. He continued,

"Highness, there can be no harm in thinking that we are the tenants of the most magnificent heavenly body at the centre of the Universe, no one alive can state otherwise with any certainty, However, a keen observer can detect that the angle of the sun varies at different periods and seasons, being more directly above us in the summer than winter. This factor alone informs us that the sun has a direct effect on the seasons on earth. This, along with other similar observations, aids my ability to navigate accurately, and therefore enables me to carry out my responsibility to Your Highness and the Church.

The King, quite obviously impressed, replied, "My dear young man, as a King I can rule the Franks, keep an eye on my treasure, and may even influence my wife to a degree, but I would never attempt to decide on the direction of two hundred and fifty ships across the sea by day and night, with no landmarks to guide me. You are doing a fine job and I assure you that you have my blessing and that of the Church.

On our arrival in Sicily, I will be departing with some of my company so there will then be room for your friends, whom I understand are placed on other ships, to re-join you on board. Should you ever decide to swear allegiance to me and the Fleur-de-lis, I would have no hesitation in knighting you and giving you an army to command, as I recognise in you the loyalty and formidable leadership qualities so necessary in that role."

Simon was overwhelmed by this royal compliment, but managed to respond, "Your Royal Highness honours me beyond all expectations. I am willing to serve you to the best of my ability and if I can assist you or France in any capacity, I am yours to command."

Simon fell silent as the cabin door behind him opened and the King and the Admiral rose to greet the four ladies. The King smiled and gestured to his queen to take the seat beside him.

Simon's immediate reaction was to ask permission to take his leave, but before he had a chance, the King raised his hand and said," Simon, I would like to introduce you to my Queen, to whom you have already spoken, Lady Louise is her companion, Princess Alice our beloved sister with Lady Sarah her friend and companion. Ladies, this young gentleman, whom you have already met, is Simon the navigator, who will guide us safely to our destination. It is he, I would like to appoint as Companion Protector to Princess Alice, when we part company with her and Lady Sarah on our arrival in Sicily."

Simon could not have been more surprised. He knew that Princess Alice was on board the Bella Doria, with her brother King Philip and his Queen. He had learnt this when he bid 'bon-voyage' to his good friend Pierre. While Pierre had been reconciled with his brother Philip, who had re-instated his title 'Prince', he had chosen to avoid his sister, Alice, and travel instead with King Richard.

Without pausing, Princess Alice stepped forward and spoke: "I am so pleased to meet you **Sir** Simon the Navigator."

Simon was frozen to the spot. He bowed towards the Queen and her husband, but was too shocked to turn and face the ladies, as etiquette demanded. Alice held out her hand to Simon with a warm smile and then turned her attention to her brother. Her one word had challenged the King, who looked inquiringly at his Queen. She responded readily, "I fully agree with the Princess. Her appointed protector has, at the least, to be a noble Knight."

The King looked perplexed and explained that he had already offered a Military Command and due honours, were Simon to swear allegiance to France. As he had declined and had never stepped foot on Frankish soil, to bestow a knighthood without the approval of a royal commission would be difficult, if not impossible, to justify and would cause considerable opposition from other Noblemen.

But Princess Alice stubbornly insisted, "If I am to have a protector other than my Liege, he has to be a Nobleman. It has always been so – it is the tradition".

The silence that followed was palpable.

Then a sudden thought came to Simon which gave him the courage to break the icy spell.

"Sire, if I may make a suggestion?"

The King waved his assent. "It may be possible to resolve this impasse by looking outside France but remaining within your authority. A rebellious prince, a Frankish nobleman, one Isaac Comnenus, has declared himself King of the island of Cyprus, in rebellion against Byzantium. This could be interpreted as putting the island under your authority. I believe that in the east of the island there was once a great city called Salamis, which now stands in ruins, half covered in sand. In its day it was a city renowned for its wealth of art and was an important centre of trade, but now it is deserted and so there is no-one there to take offence if I were made a Knight of Salamis.

The King looked around him and saw only unanimous approval and gradually the worried lines turned to a happy smile.

Princess Alice was delighted with the satisfactory solution. The King rose and stood before Simon resting his hands on the young man's shoulders in a friendly gesture, "Young Simon, you navigate the troubled waters of diplomacy with the same extraordinary skill with which you navigate your fleet. On our arrival in Sicily, you will be duly knighted in the presence of King William, and may God bless you and be with you always."

As the lady Louise followed the royal couple out of the

cabin, Princess Alice walked over and offered her hand to Simon, in the manner of the royals ahead. He sheepishly offered the back of his hand on which she gently placed the tips of her fingers and so together they followed the others out of the cabin. Lady Sarah was partnered by the Admiral and did not look at all happy with the new arrangements. The King and Queen led them to the dining room and as the Princess approached her seat next to the Queen, she indicated to Simon to take the place next to her. Simon at first hesitated, but noticing the expectations of the others he accepted without more ado, but the discomfort of Lady Sarah, in his presence, did not escape his notice.

At the outset Simon planned to limit his contact with the Princess to a minimum but he found her determined to be in his company on every possible occasion. Remembering Pierre's stories about his sister, he was only too aware of the possible danger of this close proximity. But she was, after all, a very exceptional lady, a very attractive Princess with the gift of a sharp brain, a ready wit and a bright intelligence enhanced by the benefit of an excellent education. Above all she had an ease with all around her and a complete absence of snobbery. For all this, Simon held her in high esteem. Lady Sarah, however, while possessing similar beauty and the natural elegance of the Princess and enjoying high status at court, seemed very conscious of her position and felt a constant need to justify it, often at the expense of her companions. Simon took great care to protect himself, and not make mental contact with those around him. He confined his telepathy to conversations with his parents. Recent communications with home had been encouraging. He had learnt that his old teacher, Musa, had been summoned to the court of Sultan Saladin, to join his advisory team, called to formulate a strategy against the formidable force approaching them. They understood, without doubt, from previous experience that the sole aim of the Crusade was the total destruction of all that was alien to their stated beliefs.

Nearer at hand, however, Simon could detect internal power struggles and intrigues within the Crusader cause itself, and these disruptive factions could seriously damage the chances of the venture's success.

On a personal level the journey's end in Sicily could easily prove problematical for the strategically planned marriage of the Frankish Alice to Richard, King of England, particularly if the rumours of his father's earlier dalliance with his betrothed had reached Richard's ears. Though appearing to have been made in a political heaven, the proposed alliance could easily turn to disaster.

Simon suspected that even the Admiral of the Fleet had his own agenda and any decision he made would be biased in favour of Genoa.

Simon, it seemed, was alone in having no personal ambition and no intention of acting in any way other than impartially and loyally, and to the best of his ability.

The voyage south was calm and generally uneventful. Simon's contact with the royal party increased daily, especially with the Princess. However, on one particular evening, Sarah, who previously had appeared to be avoiding Simon's company, expressed a concern over a pain in her right shoulder and hinted that she would appreciate it if Simon were able to ease her predicament.

To his intense embarrassment Simon realised that in spite of his care, the tale of his exploits, particularly the healing of the Padre, was more widely known than he had wished. He rather reluctantly agreed to help her, knowing that it would demonstrate to them all, his special gift. He had her sit upright facing directly ahead. He stood a respectable distance behind her and stretched out his hand towards her shoulders. Sensing the tightness in her neck muscles, he searched her mentally to discover the cause. He found a bruised bone that had affected the cartilage in her shoulder joint. This had sent a pain signal down the sensory nerve. Simon quickly identified the cause to be the narrowness of Sarah's bed, due to the restricted space in her sleeping quarters and the possibility that she was resting her shoulder on her pillow rather than her head and neck. Simon, using his finger tips and mental powers moved a small amount of fatty tissue into a cushioning position, to ease the pressure on the damaged bone. He then manipulated the tendons to relieve the tension and suggested she altered her sleeping position and keep level and upright for the rest of the day. The growing smile on her beautiful face was a clear indication to all of her improved condition. The other ladies were amazed by the immediate cure as they had seen nothing like it before and thought it must be either a miracle or magic. The Queen was the first to speak, "What would you say if I were to appoint you as our Royal Physician, Simon?"

"I would be very honoured, Highness, but can you imagine the response to such an appointment, particularly from your other Physicians? The Church would demand an explanation, as it is the Church that provides the training for all the physicians in Christendom, and no answer could be forthcoming. May I instead suggest that this incident be kept within this company and I assure you that my personal skills will be available at any time, to all of you here now."

But Simon was disturbed. He was not happy that an increasing number of people appeared to know of his special powers. Also he had found when treating Sarah that as he probed to discover the source of her ills he had suddenly encountered her thought patterns, which he instantly blocked from his mind, but not before realising the complexities of life for a lady in her privileged position in the royal court.

Later that evening he escorted the Princess and Lady Sarah to their cabin in silence.

It was planned for King Richard to replenish his fleet in Reggio de Calabria, on the Italian mainland, and then proceed to Limassol in Cyprus, before arriving in the Holy Land.

Meanwhile Philip Augustus' armies and all that accompanied them had to be provided for in Sicily and provisioned for the long voyage to Acre. There they would join Richard and Leopold of Austria, to embark on the enterprise, later to be named in history as 'The King's Crusade'. The four united armies would spearhead the attack against Saladin (Selah ad Din Yusuf bin Ayyub), and aim to reinstate Guy de Lusignan as King of the Holy Land.

With the expected arrival of Frederic Barbarossa, all the senior Royal families of the Christian world would be seen there, showing their support for this venture.

Simon was busy. He had to deploy the vessels in his care to various harbours around the island of Sicily, according to the ability of these resorts to supply sufficient replenishment to the fleet to allow it to accomplish the onward journey in relative comfort.

His aristocratic passengers on the Bella Doria were destined for the port of Messina, where they would be hosted by King William and his queen, Joan, who was a sister of King Richard.

Very important negotiations were due to take place in Messina at that time. It was planned to draw up the guidelines for the division of authority across Christian Europe that would result in a declaration of Papal support for the candidate for the new Holy Roman Emperor.

A large number of sea gulls had adopted the armada, seeing it as a ready source of food, and Simon used them to obtain useful information about his surroundings and the other vessels in his care.

One evening, as he watched the gulls leave after their daily forage in the wake of the ship, he detected a distortion along the line of the horizon to the east. The following morning the Italian mainland came into view and as the day wore on it became increasingly interesting to the passengers.

Later that day Simon had lit the lanterns above his desk and was enjoying the solitude of his cabin. This was his most private place where no-one would intrude and where he could communicate with his parents without fear of interruption. The earlier wind at twilight had calmed down to a mere breeze that rocked the boat gently as a cradle. Simon, exhausted from his day's deliberations, sank back in his chair and took his flute from his inside pocket. Before he could play a note his eyes closed and the last thing he remembered was his wish to erase all the stresses of the day and sink into oblivion. He had so many questions to answer but before he could make any decisions about his personal life he had fallen into a deep sleep.

The next thing he heard was a knock on his cabin door. He was surprised to find the heat of the next day had already built up in the cabin and he was uncomfortably warm. It was the Admiral at the door and he greeted Simon, "You are taking your responsibilities far too seriously, dear friend. You must learn to control your level of commitment if you intend to live a long and fulfilled life. Do you remember the first time we met in the Council Chamber in Genoa? When I stood to address the Consulate I was intending to make an entirely different speech. I am convinced, to this day, that the entire council was surprised by my offer, but I have never regretted anything that I have committed to then or since our association. I have been thinking about this for some time and I feel you have a strange influence over me, but always for good and I would very much like to extend our relationship by offering you a partnership in my company."

The offer was so unexpected that Simon was at a loss to know how to answer, yet he knew that this was not to be his destiny.

"Admiral, I respect you, and you have my loyalty as my Captain and my friend, but what you are offering is well beyond my aspirations. While I thank you for your generosity I feel that the venture we are both bound to leaves us little room to plan ahead."

Not wishing to appear dismissive of the honour his friend had paid him he added,

"Perhaps, when this present undertaking is nearing its conclusion I may be able to judge more clearly my plans for the future. However, friend, right now, I think we both need breakfast!"

The Admiral appreciated Simon's honesty and was about to leave the cabin when he noticed Simon's flute,

"I was not aware of your love of the flute. I also play and perhaps one day we may play together."

Simon did not consider himself a performer but answered, "I would like that very much but the music I play is very personal and I fear it may not be so entertaining for others."

"We shall find that out soon enough but now we should join the others for breakfast."

The Royal family and their company had already enjoyed a hearty meal, their appetites enhanced, as usual, by the sea air.

The King, conscious that their voyage was almost over and the following day they would be leaving the ship, took the opportunity of thanking the Admiral, Simon and all the sailors for an excellent and very memorable journey. He hoped that the parting would only be temporary and that they would all meet again at their final destination.

The Admiral responded on behalf of all, assuring the King that it had been an honour to serve the Royal family and their entourage. He thanked them for the memories they had provided that would be cherished and he hoped to be of service again in the future.

That evening, being the last on board, there was a

party atmosphere and the meal was served in the open air on the deck between the aft and mid castles, the area set aside as a place of leisure for the royals. The dinner had been prepared with extra care and pleasant conversation flowed freely alongside a plentiful supply of good wine. When the Admiral produced his flute and asked the King's permission to play, the approval was unanimous and the King gestured the Admiral to proceed.

The first, a classical tune from Geneve's Harmonious Expressions was followed by a very fast-moving jig that sounded nautical, but Simon could not place it. It certainly had a pace that had all the company tapping their feet. It was met with whole-hearted appreciation as it came to an end.

The Queen was the first to inquire as to the origin of the unusual, lively piece. The Admiral, proud of the interest the Queen had shown, was happy to share the history of the tune. It was music favoured by fishermen from the Pontus region. These fishermen, often numbering as many as twenty to a long and narrow boat, could be out at sea for many days at a time. To amuse themselves and to stretch their legs in the narrow confines of their boat, they developed a dance of fast steps that they performed on the centre beam above the keel and within the standing space of each individual, in order to avoid rocking the boat. It was a remarkable sight and sound, even when they practised it on land.

Hoping to witness such an event the Queen then enquired if any of those fishermen would be joining the Crusade. However, the Admiral thought it highly unlikely, as they were a small community and their families depended almost entirely on their fishing. Their land was near the mountains and poor so farming was limited and only hazelnut trees grew in abundance on the mountain slopes. The men were needed in the village to support the community.

Simon appeared to be in deep thought as he gazed at the horizon, disrupted by the silhouette of Sicily. In fact he was avoiding any contact with Princess Alice. A tug on his sleeve returned him to the gathering. Apparently, the Admiral had informed everyone about Simon's mastery of the flute and it was his turn to entertain. The expectations of the assembled group left him no means of possible escape, so he took out his flute and without thinking, started playing a tune that he had never heard before. It was in perfect harmony with the night, the gentle roll of the vessel, the calm of the sea, the brilliance of the stars above and the warmth he felt towards the company. When he finished his recital, all was quiet for a moment until the Princess started clapping and so broke the spell. All then joined in enthusiastic applause.

The Queen then turned to her ladies, "Ladies, it is now your turn to perform to complete the night's entertainment. Go fetch your mandolins and remind us of the music of our beloved France."

They returned with finely decorated instruments which they played with accomplished skill. The Prelude that they played was followed by a beautiful French song performed as a duet, which formed a fitting end to the evening's entertainment. Gradually they all drifted to their cabins happy but conscious that from the following day their lives would be very different.

Breakfast the next morning was a quiet affair but taken in good spirits. Everyone was occupied with their own thoughts.

The King was contemplating the important treaty he was expecting to sign with King William and the secret agreement regarding Frederic Barbarossa. The Queen was feeling disappointed that she would not have the opportunity to build a relationship with Queen Joan, Richard's sister and Queen of Sicily, who would be boarding the Bella Doria, to meet Princess Alice and escort her to her brother Richard in Acre, where the two were to be wed. Alice, anxious that her reputation may have preceded her, was planning how she could impress Queen Joan. All her training had instilled in her the importance of first impressions. She had to prove herself to be a good choice as Queen of England, without alienating other ladies already close to the King.

King Philip, anxious to be about his business, enquired of the Admiral their anticipated schedule for arrival and was informed that within the half hour the harbour pilot would be alongside to escort them to their allocated berth. The King then added,

"I shall be expecting your presence when I bestow the Knighthood on Simon at the Palace, then later tonight we shall all enjoy a farewell supper."

At that point Simon approached the King and begged permission to speak.

"Go ahead, Simon, what is on your mind?"

And so Simon shared with the King the problem that was troubling him.

"Sire, when Queen Joan comes aboard tomorrow,

she will take complete command of the ladies' situation. Your generous gesture in granting me a knighthood will be rendered meaningless for the task it was intended to serve. As this is unavoidable I beg you to assign me as your representative, to oversee the ladies' need and security, as a friend, and with the explicit responsibility for ensuring the Lady Sarah's well-being, as her situation may be about to change drastically."

Casting a conspiratorial glance at his Queen the king replied,

"You seem to harbour the noblest of thoughts, Simon. My Queen and I were planning to give Lady Sarah the small town of Versailles, which is part of my personal estate, as a dowry, on her marriage to someone of our approval. If that 'someone' should be you, then the union would carry my blessing and the title of baron. However, that has given me another thought. There will be much pressing business in Sicily so why wait?"

Turning to the guard at the doorway he ordered him to fetch his sword. Simon, who had humbly knelt before the king to make his request was still kneeling when the guard returned. The King indicated he should remain in place and raising his sword, he touched Simon lightly on both shoulders, and to everyone's delight proclaimed,

"Arise, Sir Simon of Salamis!"

It took Simon less than a moment to absorb what had just passed and the enormity of the implications. When his friend, the Admiral, seeing him somewhat bewildered by the turn of events, stepped forward to offer assistance, he accepted the gesture and rose to his feet. Turning round he encountered all eyes focussing on him, expressing their approval and awaiting his reaction. He was somewhat disconcerted to see the lady Sarah curtsey towards him, with an undeniable blush.

The Queen was the first to offer her hand and Simon stepped forward gently accepting it. He brushed it with his lips and then bowed further touching the hand with his forehead, in an instinctive Islamic sign of respect. He then stepped closer to the King and repeated the obeisance.

FIFTEEN

TWISTS OF FATE

S icily proved to be a place for unexpected changes in destiny. The first news the party received on disembarking was of the death of King William some time earlier. This had left King Richard's sister Queen Joan, a widow, and had placed in possible jeopardy the secret Papal negotiations over the new Holy Roman Emperor. King Richard, on hearing the news and being already in the vicinity, had immediately arrived to take charge of proceedings. He had arranged for the Sicilian Royal treasury to be removed and stored for his sister's safe keeping on board his largest vessel.

He had also received entirely reliable information that his intended bride, Princess Alice, had been compromised by his father King Henry. This abominable act further justified his long-standing hatred of his father and gave Richard cause to immediately announce the breaking of his betrothal to Alice.

Richard had not waited even to meet Alice or inform the French King of his intentions towards his sister, but had sent word to his mother whom he had always turned to for support. Queen Eleanor, hearing of Princess Alice's demise, and concerned for the future happiness of her son, suggested her own protégé, the Princess Berengaria of Navarre as a suitable wife for Richard and queen for England. Richard, relying, as ever, on the wise judgement of his beloved mother, and holding pleasurable memories of Berengaria as a child, accepted her proposal without hesitation and Eleanor set out on the long journey to meet him. Meanwhile, Richard, happy in the knowledge that his mother and sister would take good care of his matrimonial affairs in his absence, put behind him his personal anxieties and set sail with his armada.

When Philip arrived at the palace to a welter of unexpected and appalling news, he was furious. Unable to face his sister's humiliation and his own crushed ambitions, he promptly arranged for a suitable escort and sent Princess Alice accompanied by Lady Sarah, back to France.

He was further incensed to find that even while his sister was still ignorant of her betrothed's intentions, Queen Eleanor had arrived in Sicily accompanying Berengaria, Richard's newly intended wife.

Only the promise of ten thousand pieces of gold from Richard (most probably taken from his sister's treasury) would help assuage King Philip's anger.

Eleanor was pleased to have arrived in Messina in time to meet the fleet and so arrange passage for Berengaria to meet Richard in Acre. On being greeted by her daughter, Joan, she expressed her sympathy for her daughter's recent bereavement, and hoped she would be as happy to travel with Berengaria as she had apparently been to accompany Alice.

Joan was a handsome woman of great bearing and natural authority, traits she had obviously inherited from her mother. When Berengaria and her lady-in-waiting, Lady Loraine, were introduced to her by her mother, they were received with great courtesy. She happily agreed to travel with them and take them under her protection on the long journey ahead.

Eleanor, her task now complete, left to retrace her steps to England where she would fulfil her role as Dowager Queen beside her son King John, who ruled the country in his brother, Richard's, absence.

Without the care for their passengers, the sailors on board the Bella Doria enjoyed a few days of quiet, carrying out maintenance and re-victualing.

Finally, they were ready to set sail and with their new passengers on board, and a strong westerly wind to assist them, they left the Island of Sicily behind them.

The Frankish king, Philip Augustus would be the last to leave the island and would follow in their wake in two days' time with the support of the Spanish fleet.

SIXTEEN

PSYCHIC DEPTHS

The new passengers did not take long to settle into their new surroundings. Queen Joan was accompanied by a small group of ladies, her personal Chaplain, and a man dressed in the attire of a Templar.

The Admiral had also taken on board Simon's former companions and had found them suitable employment for the duration of their passage.

As for Simon, it was a time of deep personal reflection. Once the Lady Sarah had left with her disgraced Princess he judged that he had acted improperly. He feared that he had been too familiar and had given the wrong impression as to his intentions. He felt ashamed and vowed that he would not make the same mistake again and so would lie low and avoid all social complications. With his mind made up he strode to the Admiral's cabin to share his decision and enlist his friend's support. To his surprise his friend showed little sympathy and instead insisted that he inform the Queen at dinner that he no longer wished to hold responsibility for the well-being of the young ladies. "That is not what I intended, Admiral, but rather to avoid the royal party completely."

But the Admiral would not hear of that and in response misquoted a comment made previously by King Philip, suggesting that Simon, as a famous navigator who had steered safely through many troubled seas, should surely have no problem navigating a safe passage through his own social quandaries. Simon was not convinced and approached the evening meal with great misgivings. The evening started amicably enough. He had decided not to speak out on this occasion but to wait and see how events unfolded. He was happy when he was introduced to the honoured guests simply as Simon the Navigator. He had quietly refused wine and was congratulating himself on keeping a low profile and attracting little attention to himself by avoiding taking part in the conversation at table. He longed to be back in his cabin but protocol demanded that the Queen be first to leave the table. When she did eventually stand, she turned to address Simon by his formal title. "Sir Simon, it is our understanding that King Philip Augustus bestowed your title as Protector of the Princess Alice. As the Princess is no longer with us, we would be obliged if you would continue in the role of protector and provide escort for the Princess Berengaria and the Lady Loraine. We are conscious of your onerous responsibilities to the fleet and I give you my promise that the ladies will not distract you from your normal duties."

With a heavy heart Simon was left with no words other than, "Your Highness honours me."

All bowed as she swept from the room, with her Bishop and Knights Templar following her. The Lady Loraine moved to follow but the Princess of Navarre indicated for her to remain behind.

Berengaria then turned to Simon and addressed him with an impish smile,

"We are ready to be accompanied to our cabin, Sir Simon, and as it is on the way to your own quarters it should not distract you unnecessarily."

Acknowledging her command, he stepped over the threshold in order to assist them and led them to their quarters. He pretended not to notice the smirk on the Admiral's face as he left the dining room.

Later, retrieving a number of instruments from his work-room, Simon climbed the stairs to the aft deck to take some positional measurements and to greet the night-watch and the helmsman. He was out of sorts, finding himself thoroughly vexed by the events of the evening and worst of all he saw no way of disentangling himself without giving grave offence.

It was while he was lost in such thoughts that he became aware that he was receiving a subliminal message from an unexpected source.

"You could halve your problems by sharing them, Salem, son of Sinbad. If you were not so overwhelmed by your personal troubles you would realise that there is a whole universe out there with far greater problems and not of your making. You are a mature person now and I think it is time for you to accept your social responsibilities."

Simon immediately recognised Berengaria's voice, but was confused at first, thinking that he was dreaming. Realising that he was actually wide awake, he was astounded and had so many questions.

"Where are you speaking from? How do you know about

my origins? How did you learn to communicate with me in this manner?"

Berengaria replied with a small laugh,

"I have been reading your thoughts all evening – it is all in there! You were so pre-occupied with your personal struggles that you were ignoring everything else. Now I suggest you retire to your cabin and have good night's sleep. We should communicate in this manner every evening when we retire to our beds, where no-one can witness or disturb us. It will be our secret. Good night, Salem!"

"Good night, Princess Berengaria!"

Simon was still in a state of total shocked disbelief when he eventually fell into a deep sleep.

The next day was quiet. They received news that Richard had departed four days earlier, from the port of Candia on the Island of Crete.

The Bella Doria had been progressing well towards its next destination, with the seasonal westerly wind behaving predictably.

That evening Simon was relaxing in his cabin rocking gently in his hammock, when he allowed his thoughts to reach out and make contact with Berengaria. He found her in her cabin with Lady Loraine, both ladies engrossed in their needlework. She acknowledged his presence immediately, without being distracted from her task.

They then embarked on a conversation and a course of action that would change three lives for ever.

"I must first apologise for my manner on our encounter last evening. I was arrogant in assuming that I was the only one of the company that had been granted such gifts. As I have never before been in this situation outside my family I

have previously followed my teacher's guidance to be wary of such approaches. However, I want you to know that I feel very differently about the present circumstances and I am very happy to be communicating with a like spirit."

"There is no need to apologise, Salem. As a matter of fact you are the first person I have encountered that I could communicate with in this manner. I always considered myself a freak of nature and at times feared for the safety of myself and my family if I should be taken as a witch. You mentioned a teacher- is there schooling in this subject in your home country?"

"No such schooling that I know of. My tutor was an elderly gentleman that I encountered. He was wise and experienced and made me aware of the gift I had inherited but had not recognised. My grandfather is similarly blessed. Are any in your family like us?"

"Not to my knowledge. My first recollection of any such ability was waking in the middle of one night in panic, believing that I was in a night-mare. However, I soon realised that it was in fact my chamber companion, Lady Loraine, who was suffering the night-mare and for some reason I found myself immersed in her mind and sharing her thoughts. Terrified by the possibility of persecution by the Church for possessing evil powers I decided there and then to keep my gift secret even from my parents. Perhaps you can imagine my relief at discovering that you held similar powers."

"Your decision was undoubtedly wise as such gifts would certainly be viewed with grave suspicion."

As they conversed Simon felt a growing rapport with this unusual young woman. As she continued to share her innermost thoughts, he was consumed with the feeling that fate had destined them as soul mates.

"*Salem, I badly need you to be my secret friend with whom I can share my worries. I have not confided in any other person, but my concern about this marriage, to which I am committed, grows daily. I do so hope for a happy union with many children, yet I am afraid that this cannot happen with Richard.*"

Simon feared for his new friend's happiness and although he did not want to unduly alarm her he felt she should know something of Richard's intentions.

"*My dear Princess, I believe your concerns may be justified. I have gathered some knowledge of King Richard and while he has always behaved in an honourable manner, he fears he may have inherited his father's evil traits and so has no intention of perpetuating his father's dynasty. He feels that by not having children he can prevent the continuation of a situation that might mar the English throne for ever.*"

"*This is exactly what I sensed and caused my concern. I know I can never marry him, but I do have one possible solution but I will need your help.*"

As Simon was receiving her thoughts he felt his own psychic energy rising to a height he had never before experienced. It was clear that together they were a formidable force with the power to achieve the unimaginable.

"*Salem, can we together work a wonder for the benefit of two people who would otherwise live unhappy lives? I will not marry Richard as he cannot give me the life I have wished for. However, Lady Loraine would sacrifice much to be Richard's wife and the Queen of England. It has been* her sole ambition since childhood. I know her well and am confident that she would willingly forego motherhood for the status of Queen. You know we are very alike. We have been like sisters from childhood and are of similar appearance and stature. We are often mistaken for each other. We have similar attitudes and often think alike except on this one issue, our ambitions for our futures, which are very different. We both need to change our lives, our futures, to be happy. Is this possible? Can we do this?"

"You have the answer in your grasp, Princess. You must allow the lady Loraine to become Princess Berengaria and fulfil her life-long dream, while you take your place beside her as the lady Loraine, to attend her until the day of her marriage to Richard, which will free you to live the life you desire".

"Can this be realistically achieved, is it truly possible?"

"In my opinion it is not only possible but thoroughly desirable. But you must be completely sure that this is what both you and Loraine desire as there can be no return. It should be effected as soon as possible as you are now with people who are strangers and do not know you well and any slight changes in manner will be overlooked. People believe what they think they expect to see and no-one will ever notice the change. For both you and Loraine there may be some small memory adjustment but that will be temporary. The process will involve a complete spirit transfer. Your entire spirit with all your past life and personality will enter Loraine's body as her spirit enters yours. This will require the highest psychic energy but I feel already a massive increase of the force. Are you sure this is what you want and that this is the right time?"

"The present time must be the most suitable, we should

do it now. My mind is made up and I shall never regret it."

While Berengaria appeared silently concentrating on her embroidery, Loraine had slipped into a deep sleep. For seconds Simon and Berengaria focussed all their combined energy on the task. Had Simon been in their cabin he would have seen a pale shimmering light rise above Berengaria's head and move towards the sleeping body of Loraine. A similar glow left Loraine and crossed over to Berengaria. At the same instant both disappeared within the bodies.

"Goodnight, Lady Loraine!"
"Goodnight, Salem el Sinbad!"

Queen Joan was beginning to show signs of annoyance. She was anxious to be nearer her brother and demanded they make every effort to catch up with his fleet. She requested the Admiral's presence in her cabin and enquired after the possibility of more speed. The admiral assured her that the ship was on course and making good progress towards their destination. He explained that were they an individual vessel it might be possible for them to travel a little faster but, as part of a large fleet, it was their responsibility to maintain the schedule. Richard however, had no such restrictions and was racing to his destination. But the Queen was not satisfied and argued that as all the ships had experienced captains who were very familiar with those waters, they were capable of following schedules without being shepherded by the Bella Doria.

The Admiral having been given a direct and royal command, had no alternative but to inform the Queen respectfully, that he would signal the fleet to avoid any confusion and make all haste to reach Richard.

The Admiral withdrew from the royal presence and went in search of Simon, whom he found in the company of his old campaign friends. He appeared to be in the process of introducing them to the Lady Loraine in whose company he seemed to be spending an increasing amount of time. On seeing the Admiral approaching, all nodded their respects and withdrew, leaving only Simon and Loraine with the Admiral. He acknowledged the men's salutes in the normal manner and then informed Simon and Loraine of Her Majesty's directive. After a moment's worried hesitation he added,

"In my experienced opinion, the only way to improve our speed in the present conditions is to utilise the temperature differences between the sea and the landmass. However this would require us to sail nearer the land and what we would gain in speed we would lose in the extra distance travelled. Simon felt that would be an acceptable option.

"The Royal Lady will be pleased to feel the wind in her hair. The only forfeit will be our contact with the rest of the fleet, which she seems happy to accept. I shall prepare the new course for the helmsman."

Having conveyed his respects to the Queen by way of the Admiral, Simon took his leave.

The Padre, who had been nearby, followed Simon and Loraine to the chart room. As Simon held the door for them to enter, he realised that he had spent very little time with Dominic over the past days and was surprised by how much he had missed his close company. He wondered how his new relationship with Loraine might affect his friendship with Dominic. But, Loraine, reading his thoughts, silently assured him that she certainly had no problem with a three-way friendship. Consoled by this, he spent the next hour happy in their company as he plotted the charts for the next stage of their journey.

Three days passed before the Queen sent for Simon. He was disappointed when she expressed grave displeasure at the progress they had made. She believed their vessel to be famed as the fastest in the fleet and did not consider that it was fulfilling its reputation. She commanded that he do whatever necessary to speed their journey. She offered the assistance of her Bishop's prayers if Simon thought that would be effective.

Simon forced a rather sarcastic reply, "We shall be grateful for all assistance, especially from the very Highest Authority, Ma'am."

The Admiral, who was also present, had been given no permission to speak, and was looking frustrated, when the Queen indicated for them to leave, by pointing imperiously at the door. Without a word they respectfully withdrew.

The Admiral, devoid of any new strategy appeared quite distraught and so in desperation decided to take advantage of the Queen's offer of prayers. He sent a message by the Padre to all the ship's company, requesting them to join the Bishop, that evening in a Mass in supplication for a favourable wind. The helmsman and the look-out in the crows-nest were the only two not invited to the prayers and as they pursued their normal tasks they observed the proceedings with very little interest.

The Bishop had positioned himself, with due ceremony, on a crimson cushion on the balcony, in full view of his gathered congregation. Just as he was about to start the Mass there was an interruption as the Queen appeared with her two guards, who carried the royal chair that they placed at the front, where the Queen indicated. The Princess and Loraine appeared, carrying their cushions and settled themselves comfortably behind the Bishop. Finally, all were ready and devout attention was focussed on the Bishop who started the Mass.

Simon, not being familiar with the prayers, was soon losing concentration, when he was shaken back to consciousness by the Lady Loraine's thoughts.

"Why not ask your friendly old Giant Rock Pine for help, Salem?"

Simon considered the wisdom of her suggestion for a moment before responding,

"It will not be easy. The concentration required to cover that distance along with the movement of the ship, may make me unsteady, and my condition may be noticed and cause concern."

"It will very soon be dark. If you can get the Padre, who is next to you, to support you, any movement would not be observed."

Simon discreetly leaned against the Padre, who, deep in prayer, appeared not to notice and held his position. Partially closing his eyes, Simon moved into a semi-trance. Oblivious of his surroundings, he allowed his thoughts to drift to the north-northwest. They carried him past the Adriatic coast-line to the Duchy of Apulia, and then guided him through the Papal State of Bologna. Beyond there he felt the closing presence of the Pine and fought mentally to make contact. The Great Pine responded, welcoming him like an old friend. When Simon explained his problem and his request, the great tree did not answer immediately. Simon waited.

"Your request may have extreme and unwelcome consequences. I can and will initiate the beginning of a squall but many other factors may influence its final force and duration."

Simon always curious and anxious to increase his knowledge and understanding of the ways of nature, asked,

"Is it possible for you to explain this process and what it involves?"

"There is a temperature change to warmer air high up in the mountains. This will destabilise the snow mass causing an avalanche which will travel along the glacier surface at very high speed, carrying extremely cold and heavy air south away from the mountains. As the much warmer air in the south is displaced by this, there will be considerable disturbances, the power of which cannot be predicted by me or any but Mother Nature herself. I can, however, assure you, that such a disturbance is moving into the vicinity of your fleet even now. May the God of Nature be always with you, Simon, my friend!"

As Simon slowly returned to the present, he felt exhausted and was surprised when Loraine told him he had been away less than an hour.

He saw from the Bishop's blessing that the Mass was about to finish and the congregation paused in quiet personal reflection.

Unwilling to impose on this special moment, Simon waited until the Queen made to move, and then raised his hand for permission to speak. The Queen affirmed with a slight nod.

"Your Highness, I believe the weather is changing and I shall need volunteers to prepare the ship for an imminent storm. I advise your royal party to return to the safety of your cabins."

The Queen again nodded her assent but could not hide the look of extreme scepticism on her face. She then signalled the end of prayers to the relief of all, especially the Bishop, with his ailing knees. He was not entirely convinced that he had played any part in this miraculous event, but, as this was not something that he would readily admit to, he welcomed the general acceptance of the value of prayer.

Simon straightened up and looked around for likely volunteers and found everyone facing him with willing expectation. He selected the most appropriate and posted the chosen sailors to particular tasks. He then proceeded to give the helmsman the new co-ordinates to maximise the anticipated winds. He scheduled himself to stand by the tiller and assist, when necessary, to ease the boat into the storm ahead and so build up the speed. They already had full canvas. Within a short period the wind had increased dramatically and the sails had to be shortened for the safety of the vessel and those on board.

All the passengers had retired to their quarters as suggested, with the exception of the old Templar, who had turned out to be her majesty's fiscal counsellor on the expedition. He staggered up to the aft-deck and approached Simon who was standing by the helmsman.

He took Simon by the arm and steered him out of the earshot of others suggesting to Simon that this was not to be a casual, social chat.

The Templar introduced himself as Signor Marcos and admitted that he had been observing Simon on the instructions of the Grand Master. The Order had been aware of Simon for some time and he had, in fact, been most impressed with what he had seen, both the personable manner and the obvious leadership skills. He would therefore be recommending to the Order that they give Simon every assistance, to further his ambitions.

He added, "I value our acquaintance and am looking forward to enhancing it on this journey."

Simon, who had acknowledged the greeting but had refrained from further comment finally answered, "I shall look forward to that pleasure, Sir Knight."

Signor Marcos nodded again as he turned and headed towards his quarters in the mid-castle, as the pressure of the wind in their sails catapulted them towards the south-east.

At that moment Simon had another idea to maximize the forces of nature. He considered the possibility of riding a wave. If he could maintain the pace of the wave it should be possible and it would avoid the buffeting between the highs and lows of troughs. He helped the helmsman steer to the right and timed the next wave. He felt the boat rise with the wave and perch on its crest. This was a peculiar sensation, totally transforming their movement. It felt that time, for them, was stationary while all around them was turmoil.

All on board were conscious of the change but only the experienced sailors could identify the fantasy of it.

The Admiral, uneasy at such a wild risk, met Simon at the helm and challenged the wisdom of not reducing sail as was commonly practiced in such circumstances.

At that moment Simon became conscious of Loraine's remote presence. Mentally shadowing him from Berengaria's cabin, she knew he was burdened and needed her support. Her added strength enabled Simon to respond to the Admiral without losing control of the proceedings.

"We shall be encountering much more powerful winds before long. If we abandon the opportunity to maintain our present position, we may find ourselves at the mercy of the storm without any control of the outcome. In our present situation it may be possible to avoid the worst".

The Admiral was not entirely convinced,

"I am prepared to support your judgement as always, my friend. May God be with us all!"

At sunrise the sky was cloudless and the visibility was only marred by the rise of gigantic waves. They had steered a path to the east, gliding on the crest of the wave that was travelling at an incredible speed and would carry them well east of Crete.

Simon and Lady Loraine were now inseparable, periodically transferring control of events from one to the other, to ease the stress and ensure the safety of all. They were in perfect harmony, their intimacy was beyond perception and the bond they had created was incomparable.

By noon, the sky above was covered with a reddish cloud that had grown gradually and was obscuring the view to the south. This phenomenon was brought to the attention of the Queen who turned to her learned Bishop for an explanation. She found him at a loss and so sent for the Admiral, who had already discussed the sight with Simon and so was well prepared to answer her. "Your majesty, we are of the opinion that this strange colouration of the atmosphere is caused by minute particles of sand that have been carried on the wind from the African desert to the south of us. It is quite a natural occurrence".

But the Queen was not satisfied. She knew that the storm winds were coming from the north, so how could it be that the sand was being carried on a wind from the south. Eventually, Simon was sent for and asked to fully enlighten the company. His first thought was not to cause any challenge to the clergy and glancing across at the Bishop he said,

"With respect Ma'am, this is God's way of balancing forces within His domain."

Having just heard a similar comment from her Bishop the Queen feared she was being humoured and very nearly lost her patience.

"Sir Simon, I am not prepared to accept unsubstantiated explanations from either you or the Bishop and I now expect from you something more plausible."

"Your Highness, our highly respected Bishop was guiding you in good faith. However, a demonstration may serve to prove a more acceptable and detailed answer. I will only require a large bowl with water and some rose petals." The Queen turned to Loraine and sent her off to collect all that Simon needed. Loraine soon returned with two maids, carrying between them a large bowl, a pitcher of water and a container of dried rose petals, which they placed on the table in the centre of the cabin. The Queen then directed her attention to Simon, who moved forward confidently to carry out his demonstration.

"Your Highness, the water in this bowl will represent the sea. On one side I shall introduce these petals which will behave like the air above the sea on the northern shores of Africa. When cold water, acting as the cold air coming down from the north, is added to the opposite side of the bowl, we notice that the rose petals travel north, against the flow of the water, despite my attempts to blow them back to the other shore. In nature the heavy cold air from the north is coming past us and pushing the warmer, lighter air in the south up into the atmosphere. This raises the fine sand into the upper air and then carries it north at a higher level above the cold air. The falling rain will eventually wash these particles from the atmosphere or, being heavier than air they will fall and settle."

As Simon moved his finger beneath the water, the petals again moved in the opposite direction.

The Queen was delighted and her previously expressionless face beamed with a wide smile of approval. She had been impressed by the demonstration and thanked Simon warmly.

Simon, knowing that the storm was likely to grow even more violent, recommended that everyone still stay within the safety of their cabins.

The combined mental efforts of Simon and Loraine had been employed in holding the ship on the wave and exercising some control over the storm, but now they were both exhausted and their psychic capacities totally drained. Nature took over and the tempest raged with increased fury.

The rain was torrential and the uncontrolled ship plunged into seemingly bottomless troughs between the mountainous waves that swept over the decks. The unfortunate sailors whose tasks required them to be on deck were lashed to the boat by strong ropes, but even then their physical exhaustion was rendering them vulnerable to danger. They had reduced the sail to an absolute minimum, barely adequate to assist the steering and the Admiral had accepted Simon's recommendation to order hourly watch periods to ease the fatigue of the men on deck. Fortunately the rain and waves had washed the vessel clean of the slimy, brown sludge, left by the sand on the deck.

At times the sea seemed to be above them as much as around them. The strong timbers of the sturdy Bella Doria withstood the pressure imposed on them with little more than a creak but as to their co-ordinates even Simon could only hazard a guess.

One day merged into the next and time became irrelevant. Their only aim was to survive. Simon, eventually estimated that they should be somewhere south west of the island of Cyprus, an island named by the Assyrians as Cuprum, due to the richness of copper in the land there. He instructed the helmsman to steer south east anxious to avoid any possible land while they were still not in control of the ship.

The helmsman responded to orders but immediately reported a total loss of steering. Anxious not to distress others unnecessarily, Simon kept that information to himself in the hope that circumstances would soon improve.

Miraculously, as suddenly as the storm had risen, it abated. The fury of the wind dropped to a gentle breeze, the mountainous waves calmed to a moderate swell and the visibility became crystal clear. The horizon, that not so long ago held many invisible hazards, then presented a sandy beach that stretched into the distance to the west and the curve of a protected cove ahead of them.

Everyone rushed to the top deck almost in disbelief but within moments this was replaced by joy at the prospect of a safe landing. As the midday sun's warmth dispersed the few remaining clouds leaving a perfect, blue sky, they were all glad to be alive, with their future safety relatively assured.

The Admiral, on ultimately being informed about the state of the tiller, ordered a controlled approach to the shore and the anchor dropped in a suitable, low water location to allow for inspection and facilitate repairs.

Two divers went below the ship to investigate and soon surfaced to report the sheering off of a kingpin that secured the main part of the rudder to the rest of the boat. As they carried no replacement on board, it would require the assistance of a blacksmith and his forge. This left them with no option but to go ashore and seek assistance from the local community.

The Queen summoned her two senior officers for a report on the situation. On hearing that they must land, she was most anxious to be assured that it was a Christian country. The Admiral appeared to be well briefed.

"Yes, Ma'am, to the best of our knowledge it has a reputation of being the first country to have officially accepted Christianity. It has been part of the Eastern

Roman Empire under the rule of Byzantium in Constantinople. Their Governor is a French Nobleman called Isaac Comnenus."

"The name is familiar. I believe he is related to my late husband, the King. I suggest you send a herald to him immediately requesting his presence and urgent assistance and so enable our journey to proceed without delay."

The Admiral decided to stay on board to supervise the general repairs necessitated by the damage caused by the storm. Simon was designated to lead the landing party that left in the longboat. He had selected his friends from the Genoese guard to accompany him and some of the Portuguese sailors to man the boat. When the Admiral looked questioningly at his choice, he explained, "I am anxious about the degree of hospitality to expect from the locals. This island is very close to diverse political influences and it is difficult to determine where their true loyalties lie."

"Remind everyone you come across that all involved in the Holy Crusade have the freedom of passage in all the lands of Christendom and are entitled to seek and receive reasonable assistance. Above all stress that we do carry Royal passengers."

"We shall do our utmost to summon urgent assistance but we have no-one among us that wears the emblem of a Crusader".

It was the Templar that stepped forward, "Then I had better volunteer."

The old Knights Templar took the bench in the fore of the boat in full view of anyone on land. As the oarsmen eased the boat towards the not so distant shore, Simon acknowledged the salute of the Admiral and the waves of the ladies from the mid castle. Then addressing the crew, "Together again lads! I very much hope that the rest of our journey is more pleasant. Shall we offer prayers for that Padre?"

"We should always pray for a safe return to our loved ones, Simon."

"Amen to that!" was the general response as winks and smiles passed among the friends who were obviously elated at being together again and confident that in this company they could handle any predicament that fate threw at them.

On the sandy beach of their chosen landing site, a small gathering of men and women was approaching, apparently, in order to welcome them. Signor Marcos raised his right hand and turned his palm to the rear in a gesture of greeting. Simon signalled the oars to go in deep to bring the boat to a halt, as the gathering on shore appeared to be enthusiastically waving them to come ashore. The Signor waited for Simon to reach his position at the front of the boat and said,

"I believe that all is not as it appears. My instincts warn me of hidden dangers. What do you think?"

Simon mentally scanned the beach and confirmed the presence of about fifty poorly armed men hiding behind the dunes waiting to surprise the landing party.

"Your caution does you credit, Signor, there is, indeed a planned ambush, although, with our superiorly trained men and the right tactics, I believe we have the advantage of them. I do not sense any archers among them and they will not risk endangering their own kinsfolk. It is however, my wish that we should avoid violence at all costs and make every effort to befriend these people". The listening sailors sounded their agreement with the chorus,

"No blood must be shed!"

Appropriate instructions were issued as they beached the boat. The Templar in his white robe showing the red Crusader Cross, walked towards the welcoming crowd. The three sailors and Simon followed close behind calling out greetings in Italian and Levant. The rest stayed on the boat, as if readying for departure. The three and Simon casually mingled with the locals as Signor Marcos tried to communicate with them. But before he had received any intelligible response, the four had drawn their swords and taken control of the crowd. The other sailors, with the exception of the Padre, rushed to reinforce the efforts of their fellows and surrounded all before they could recover from their surprise. Simon had walked back to assist Dominic and the couple left guarding the boat, to drag it higher up the beach, when he turned to witness the approach of the ambush party, armed with a variety of implements and make-shift weapons, emerging from the bushes and from behind the dunes.

Signor Marcos raised his right hand and indicated to the approaching mob to disarm before coming nearer. They halted their already hesitant approach and looked to their apparent leader, a big burly fellow and best armed with a clumsy-looking and unwieldy sword. After a moment's consideration, he thought better of an attack, dropped his sword by his feet, and walked away from it. The rest of his band followed suit with very little hesitation.

Simon, sheathing his sword approached the old

Templar who also had sheathed his long, heavy sword and they then addressed the leader of their adversaries.

Can you explain the reason for the deceitful way you welcomed us?" enquired Signor Marcos.

"Strangers only come to us from sea or land for one purpose, to do us harm. When soldiers come along, they say they represent the King and take away what they want and call it taxation; they take our young men and call it conscription. When the pirates come they take everything they wish including our women and young girls. There is not much we can do against the soldiers but against the intruders from the sea we do anything we can to protect ourselves. If you find this deceitful then maybe that is what it is."

He had communicated his pitiful tale in a language called Romega, which appeared to be a mixture of eastern Mediterranean languages dominated by Slavic-Greek and Byzantine-Italic.

"Your logic is reasonable and you have our sympathy. As to our purpose here, we have no demands on your community other than to request the assistance of a blacksmith to carry out necessary repairs on our ship. We shall gladly pay for any services that you may provide."

"We do have a small forge in our hamlet and I am the blacksmith and am willing to help you in any way possible."

The sailors had already released the group they had held in custody and, taking their lead from the Padre, were gathered round them in friendly conversation. Only the two guarding the boat had stayed at their post, in view of the Bella Doria, in case they should be needed, back on board.

The Admiral had turned the ship round with the help of the other longboat and settled her on a sandbank, to allow access for repairs at low tide. In the meantime, the carpenter and his assistant were dealing with damage to the structure.

The landing-party had ascertained that the ruler of the land was, indeed, Isaac Comnenus, Governor of Tarsus in the Lower Armenian Kingdom of Byzantium. He was sent to Cyprus as Governor, but on arrival had proclaimed himself, King of the island and Byzantium had not been in a position to dislodge him.

"This Isaac must be a very ambitious man, which could make him dangerous. We shall have to handle him with due caution," observed the Templar.

Simon then returned to the Bella Doria to report their findings to the Queen and the Admiral.

"I believe this Comnenus to be a nephew of my late husband. I am certain that he will be happy to help us. We must convey to him news of our presence and circumstances without delay. Sir Simon, you will be our emissary and my lord Bishop will accompany you."

SEVENTEEN

ON THE ISLAND OF CYPRUS

Next morning, hurried footsteps on the upper deck woke Simon from a restless sleep. He washed and dressed quickly and went out into the brilliant sunlight. He shielded his eyes and followed the gaze of the others already on deck. On the beach he saw an assortment of folk in a variety of uniforms, some were on horseback and all with some sort of weapon. The appearance was decidedly threatening. He found the Captain and the Admiral alongside him in deep speculation at the sight ahead.

The Admiral ordered the dispatch of a boat with the Captain on board with a small group of men, to investigate, and deal with the situation as he found appropriate.

The party soon returned bringing with them a representation from the gathering on the shore. The obvious leader of the group was recognisable by the scroll he was ostentatiously carrying, as if it were a baton of authority. He was inflated with pride, being the man assigned to this important commission. He found the climb to the deck rather difficult due to the slight sway of the ship, but ignored the helping hand from one of his companions and stepped on to the deck without asking the customary permission. He strode across to the Admiral and arrogantly demanded an explanation of the Emblem of the Crusader Cross, and the Flag of the Royal House of the Kingdom of Sicily. The Admiral confirmed the Royal standard under which the ship sailed, carefully explaining that they were carrying royal passengers and that their vessel was part of a large expedition that would make history.

The explanation appeared to be far beyond the comprehension of the, until then, proud emissary. He was not prepared for dealing with persons of such education and eminence. After some time of obviously confused and stressful silent deliberation, he recovered his composure sufficiently to announce.

"I shall return to Limassol, with this information, but in the meantime I order you not to depart from your present anchorage until you receive further instructions. As for the protection claimed for the Crusader Cross it has no standing on this island and will receive no special privileges." So saying he gathered his party around him and gingerly disembarked.

When the Queen was informed of the incident, she called all her advisors to her, and enquired of each their assessment of the morning's events. The Admiral was the first to respond,

"Your highness, I found the messenger patronising and ill-prepared for Your Majesty's presence. I also detected a degree of animosity, possibly due to the man's lack of confidence in his position."

The Bishop was concerned that although the country

was almost certainly Christian, the emissary indicated no respect for the Crusader Emblem. Simon, in total agreement with the others, recommended prudence and restraint. As their main priority was to carry out repairs to their ship they should bide their time until they received a further message of intent from Limassol, or until their ship was again seaworthy. He further suggested to the Queen that should there be a request from Limassol for her royal presence, she should oblige them, but take with her only a minimal escort, that included himself, just enough to ensure her safety. Everyone else should stay on board and prepare the vessel for an immediate sailing, on the Queen's return. He added, as an after-thought that were they to be detained for any undue length of time, then the Admiral was to take all steps to locate Richard and seek his assistance.

The Queen then asked if it was possible for Simon to use his remarkable navigational skills to find Richard's whereabouts.

"I can estimate the position of Richard's armada at the beginning of the storm, but his present location depends on his captain's decisions in the circumstances. I imagine they have searched for a safe haven in the coves of one of the many islands in the Aegean or on the western shores of Asia Minor, although I suspect he may have avoided the mainland. There are not so many islands that could offer harbour protection to a fleet of that size. I shall assess this situation more thoroughly when I return to my cabin."

The Queen, not entirely satisfied, had little choice but to accept Simon's response.

Simon led the way out of the cabin with the others

following in his wake. As he approached his own cabin he felt the Admiral's friendly hand on his shoulder as he wished him good fortune. Simon thanked him with a smile.

Throughout the morning Simon had been conscious of Loraine's undeviating presence. She seemed to be in total agreement with him in all his decisions with the exception of the one that excluded her from accompanying him on the island. She did not wish to be separated from him but he convinced her that he needed her on the Bella Doria to inform him of any developments on board, when necessary, and to relay any of his messages to the Admiral.

When Simon reached the privacy of his cabin he decided that it was perhaps the right time to seek help from his old tutor, Musa, whom he knew was in the service of Sultan Saladin, and would almost certainly be gathering considerable information about the positions of the various approaching fleets.

After lengthy discussions they reached the conclusion that the most likely action of Richard was to have headed for harbour on the island of Rhodes. If that proved to be the case, it would not be easy to contact him quickly. Having thanked his old friend for his counsel and disconnected the contact, he felt exhausted by the day's exertions and fell into a light doze.

He was startled awake by a sharp knock on his cabin door.

A seaman informed him that a new emissary had arrived, directly from the King, and was seeking an audience with Queen Joan. After an invigorating splash of cold water on his face, Simon hurriedly joined the

Admiral and the Captain to receive the newcomer who had just climbed aboard. He appeared to be more familiar with expected protocol as he had asked permission before stepping on to the deck. On approaching the trio, he introduced himself and presented his credentials to the Captain, who after a cursory glance, passed them over to the Admiral. The Admiral inspected the document and then informed the messenger that he would present it to her Royal Highness.

The Queen studied the parchment and after some consideration she instructed the Admiral to inform the messenger, that in line with the request, she, along with her companions, would be ready to be escorted to meet the King after breakfast the next day.

The emissary found it hard to disguise his disappointment as he was hoping to have completed his mission within the day.

He withdrew after thanking the Queen for her audience and bowed slightly to the others.

The next morning the sun burnt brightly from a cloudless, dark blue sky, as the Queen and her companions were led through an almost deserted landscape, with fields and hillsides purple and redolent with an abundance of wild lavender. In his role as Knight Protector, Simon had placed himself directly behind the covered sedan-chair that carried Queen Joan and Princess Berengaria. The chair was mounted between two very large horses as the terrain was rough and unsuitable for a wheeled carriage.

They were expecting their journey to take about four hours. Within a short time the floral ground-cover was replaced by bushes and tall reeds, as they approached a large lake, in the middle of a flat plain, only a short distance from the sea. Simon guessed this was a salt lake which collected its water during stormy weather or when the tides were exceptionally high. He expected that this lake would dry out in the heat of the summer leaving a deposit of salt which would provide a good income for the local people.

As the royal party approached the castle in Limassol, Simon assessed that although the building was quite large, the small uncultivated courtyard suggested that this was more of a base than a royal home.

It turned out that Isaac and his family lived discreetly in the castle in Kyrenia on the north coast and used Limassol castle only when he had business in the south. They ascended steps into a spacious hallway, at the far end of which was placed a large, high-backed chair. It resembled a throne but even a casual glance revealed a hurried design and poor construction. The overwhelming sight was a massive blue banner hanging above the throne, showing an eight-sided gold star above a reclining crescent moon. Isaac had adopted this gaudy emblem as his Arms and it was believed that he had designed it himself more to impress than for its imaginative or artistic style.

In spite of this display of overt vulgarity, the newly arrived guests turned courteously to recognise the King of Cyprus, as his entrance was announced. He was of middle age and moderate stature, with the calculating air of, at best, a successful merchant, or, at worst a diabolical conspirator.

Gesturing the two ladies to comfortable chairs close to his throne, he welcomed all present without any obvious sign of enthusiasm. Simon helped the Queen and Princess to their seats and then carefully positioned himself behind them to view the hall. Comnenus addressed the Queen, "Your Majesty honours us with her presence. At any other time and in different circumstances such a visit would call for great public celebrations. Unfortunately the Crusader flag on the mast of your ship prevents this."

The Queen asked for an explanation of this remark.

"I am in a Treaty of non-aggression with the Sultan Saladin. By offering you anything other than politeness we would be in default of the terms of this treaty."

"Are the terms of this agreement, in fact, a declaration of war against the whole of Christendom, as His Holiness the Pope himself called for this Crusade?"

"I'm afraid Your Highness exaggerates. There are many in the Christian World that did not rally to the Pope's call. Many others agreed to take part in the Crusade under duress. There are also many Christians, like us, that choose to live in harmony alongside the people of Islam, as neighbours and trading partners."

"That may be, but you are putting yourself in an alliance with Islam against the Christians."

"We are certainly not in any alliance with Islam or against any realm or religion. However, we have an agreement that does not allow us to offer help to the enemies of our partners."

"That statement concedes that you are a pawn. Will you kindly state your actual intentions, Sire?"

"Your Majesty is the only Queen in this contest, but you may be surprised by the number of Kings competing for a prize that may be impossible to win. You and your entourage may depart as soon as you wish, but the Princess will have to stay as my 'visitor'."

"On what grounds do you detain her? Are you not aware that she is the chosen Queen for my brother, Richard Coeur de Lion?"

"Her presence here with me will protect us from further disturbances. Also I, too, could be looking for a queen and this Princess Berengaria would seem to be the best candidate yet. And, as for your brother, Ma'am, it is my opinion that his marriage may be very low in his priorities."

At this Simon stepped forward promptly and bowed towards the Queen, who was about to lose her royal temper, then turned on the King, "Your Highness, I am Sir Simon of Salamis. I was granted this title on being appointed as Lord Protector to the Princess Alice, by His Royal Highness, Philip, King of France. This was re-affirmed on my re-appointment by Queen Joan as protector to Princess Berengaria. In the light of this I cannot overlook your last remarks as I feel they are highly disrespectful to the princess".

"And what do you intend to do about it, Sir?"

"By the code of chivalry, I challenge you to a duel that you cannot refuse to honour, Sire!"

"Never-the-less, by the same code I can appoint a champion to fight in my place, may I not?"

"You are perfectly correct, Sire. However, when there is no longer one to take your place you will have to accept my challenge yourself."

"We have a saying in these parts 'the good can die young' and you are very young, Sir Simon."

So saying, he turned to the assembled throng, "Are any of you gentlemen prepared to be my champion?"

About half the men present stepped forward with their hands on the hilts of their swords, while the others mocked the situation.

Simon, without assessing the opposition, inquired of the King, if he should fight them all at once or one at a time.

"We shall honour the code to the letter, young man. Noble Sir Constantine is my first cousin and, while possibly the most inexperienced of my nobles, quite adequate to dispel your discontent. I am looking forward to some entertainment, so please try to make it difficult for him to kill you."

Sir Constantine, with a smile as wide as the Nile Delta, made an elaborate, theatrical bow towards the King before turning to the ladies and then all present. He approached Simon, to within two arms' length, before withdrawing his long thin sword from its scabbard and raising it above his head in salute, to loud cheering and laughter from the onlookers.

On receiving approval from the Queen and Princess, Simon joined his adversary's salute. On the touching of the two sword tips they parted to begin hostilities.

Simon instantly pirouetted clockwise on his left heel, landing on his right foot within his opponent's guard. This movement was carried out with such speed and graceful motion that it took Sir Constantine quite by surprise. The tip of Simon's sword, that had travelled full circle, at a startling rate, had come to rest within his opponent's mouth, which was just beginning to open in mesmerised astonishment and then horror. Sir Constantine's only thought was that this had to be the last act of his life. Simon's sword was resting between his opponent's lips defying any counter move. Aware that Constantine's life was entirely at Simon's mercy, every spectator as well as the combatants were frozen in time, in wrapt anticipation of the next move.

The clattering sound of Sir Constantine's sword on the wooden floor broke the spell and caused an audible gasp in the hall.

Simon, imperiously pointed his sword at his opponent indicating that he return to his original position next to a young lady whose tears were clear for all to see.

Simon then replaced his sword in its scabbard and as he did so turned, without thinking, and instinctively deflected a bolt that had been released with lethal intent, from a crossbow on the balcony. He skilfully re-directed it to the floor at the King's feet.

"I was never aware that treachery was part of the Code of Chivalry. With this kind of behaviour, I am surprised that Saladin found it appropriate to befriend you! If there are to be any other Champions, they better prepare to forfeit their lives as I am now quite spent of all compassion."

The silence that followed barely hid the obvious failure of King Isaac's bid to best the young Knight. But Comnenus was a seasoned campaigner. He raised his hand and pointed to the culprit in the balcony and ordered he be executed immediately for his unauthorised action.

That particular declaration may not have fooled many but it restored some order to the gathering.

The King, anxious to have an end to the embarrassing incident, addressed Simon in a conciliatory tone, "Sir Simon, I concede that nothing shall be imposed upon the Princess against her will. You may stay with her to ensure her safety but I warn you, I am resolved to continue to try to persuade her to become my Queen."

Simon turned towards the Queen to seek her approval for this arrangement. Receiving her agreement, he turned back to the King, "Sire, I accept your invitation, but declare that my loyalty will always be to the Princess."

"Then you shall all stay as my honoured guests until the ship is made ready to depart."

At this point the Queen intervened, "We shall require to send a lady companion here to attend to the Princess."

"That shall be my final concession. Kindly do not try my patience further, Your Highness."

With that the Royal party was shown to its quarters after what had, for them all, been a trying and tiring day.

It was the next evening when the Bella Doria was sighted bobbing on the foam in Limassol Bay. Many of the local population went out to watch its approach. The ship was brought in skilfully alongside the jetty, which reached out far from the shore, to accommodate larger vessels, because of the shallow waters of the bay.

The Admiral indicated to the harbour officials that he was seeking an audience with Queen Joan and her host, the next morning and would await a response to that effect.

Instead of the expected instructions, it was Queen Joan herself and her entourage who arrived, but without the Princess and Simon. Her Majesty, on entering her cabin, summoned the Admiral, her Bishop and Signor

Marcos, in order to acquaint them with events that had taken place on shore and to invite their counsel.

The Bishop again expressed his abhorrence at the King's indifference towards the Holy Crusade and declared that Isaac should burn in hellfire; whereas the Admiral and the Templar tried to comfort her Majesty by expressing their confidence in Simon's ability in handling difficult situations.

The Queen then chose one of her ladies to accompany Berengaria and she left immediately to attend to her new mistress. Loraine was to stay on board the Bella Doria, as Simon had suggested.

The Admiral, knowing from Simon that King Richard was most likely in Rhodes, set sail immediately to find him and deliver the news from Cyprus.

King Isaac, quite content with the course of events so far, decided to move his party to more congenial surroundings in the north, for the duration of the hot summer. His first choice was the formidable, mountain fort of Kantara. The castle perched on a rocky and impregnable ridge offered a fantastic, birds'-eye panorama of the two shorelines, for it was situated at the start of the panhandle-like peninsular which protruded east-north-east towards Syria and the Holy Land. This provided a strategic observation position against Arabic raiders arriving by sea.

Simon spotted the ruins of an ancient city far below to the south and when he inquired he learnt that it was, in fact, the remains of the city of Salamis, for which he had been named. However all the natural beauty around her meant nothing to the Princess and she refused to even dismount until Isaac offered a more suitable residence without delay.

Isaac grudgingly conceded his error of judgement and agreed to travel on to St Hilarion after a short stay for rest.

The journey to the new destination was along the northern shore of the island, on a well-used track. They passed below the construction of an Abbey and its monastery high on a ledge beneath the formidable rise of the mountain range. They were told that it was being built by the White Monks from France as a rest and rehabilitation place for the combatants in the Holy War. As they travelled, Simon, unexpectedly, felt a sudden surge of power and his sensory energy rose to a new high. Concentrating entirely on his surroundings in the hope of discovering the source of this energy, he noticed an abundance of plants with broad, flat leaves lying close to the ground, in the centre of which was a cluster of purple flowers. When he could find no other case for this surge he silently contacted his father. When hearing the description of the plant Sinbad immediately identified it as Mandrake, a plant well-known by the practitioners of the mystic arts to possess magical powers. Satisfied that he had his answer, Simon was now free to enjoy the rest of his surroundings and the profusion of carob and olives that grew naturally in the region.

On their eventual arrival at St Hilarion, after sixteen long days of travel, they found the mountain range followed the north coast of the island faithfully from east to west. The whole terrain was covered with thick pine forests and the most rugged of the peaks was crowned by a formidable array of fortifications. It was easy to recognise that the main structure had been built many years earlier and then added to over time as need required. Wherever possible the local materials had been utilised and the surrounding walls were built of natural rocks. The steep climb to the summit provided a degree of inaccessibility which not only gave security but also separated it from any local community and so the inhabitants received little help from nearby settlements.

The excellence of the domestic comfort and the magnificence of the surrounding scenery certainly compensated to some extent for the isolation and provided a degree of relaxation for both body and mind.

An excellent tourney and practice ground below the barbican was extensively used by the soldiers and guards to keep them fit and ease away the boredom of long stays of duty away from family and friends. There did not appear to be any provision of accommodation for any but the defenders themselves and the royal party.

The nearest habitable place could be seen two thousand feet below. The fortified town of Kyrenia, with its own castle and ramparts stood out proudly between two bays of the deep blue Mediterranean. In one of the bays a line of ships were harboured, completing the scene.

The unwilling guests were given apartments behind the chapel. The area was spacious and well furnished, with a large and colourfully decorated leaded glass window offering a distant view of the town and harbour below. Other accommodation, known as the Queen's apartments, were much higher up the mountain and had a fantastic view of the mountain range and sea to the west, but Simon decided that the apartment behind the chapel would be more comfortable. From there in the late evening light they were even able to see the outline of the mountain range across the sea along the southern coast of Asia Minor.

That first night, although exhausted from their travels, Simon settled down as usual to make contact with Loraine for a report of the happenings on board the Bella Doria. This contact had become much easier of late as she had occupied the cabin alone since the departure of the Princess. Simon had found that he was able to partially appear and they would practise walking around the mid-castle deck together, beyond the vision of the others, as their presence was not material but only in spirit.

EIGHTEEN

A STRANGE ENCOUNTER

On the first night at Hilarion Castle, just as Simon was preparing to reach out to Loraine, she surprised him by appearing beside him in his sleeping space, which was in an arched hallway outside the Princess's quarters. They made instant psychic contact and holding hands they left the castle, rising together through the steep crags around them. As they reached the highest peak, Simon noticed that the sea between the island and the mountains of Asia Minor, so clear when they arrived, had disappeared from existence. To the northwest they saw a cove bordered by a fantastic city, but could see no ships harboured in this natural bay.

From stories told him in his early childhood, Simon remembered the name of the fabled city of Atlantium. He was convinced that, against all logic and probability, it was that city that he was now looking down on. The view was beyond compare and like nothing either of them had ever seen before.

They watched a strange craft make its way around the mountains, gliding like a bird but without wings. It was just high enough to skim the peaks and tree tops and passed above without apparently noticing them. As it flew overhead it emitted a weird non-rhythmic note which decreased in volume as the craft cleared the mountains and sped away beyond their sight.

They looked at each other speechless and then instinctively turned their attention to the city beneath them, still holding each other's hand for reassurance, unsure of what they had witnessed.

A building that towered above all others drew their attention and without discussion they decided to investigate. The dominating building was in the shape of a pyramid which stretched up to the sky. It was undoubtedly the focal point of the community. Mentally penetrating the walls they found themselves in a massive hall in the midst of a lecture or symposium where an urgent discussion was taking place. They immediately recognised that the creatures they were observing, although in many ways resembling themselves, also exhibited some marked differences. As they moved, they seemed to glide across the floor effortlessly with no bending at the knee. They communicated with each other without the use of audible sound but Simon and Loraine found it easy to understand the interchange by intercepting the telepathy. It was a clear indication to them that thoughts need no language and where there is no language there is no misinterpretation.

It was obvious that the group was planning some sort of project and while the leader seemed in some ways indecisive, he was issuing directives on future action. On one point he appeared adamant- the colour of the skin and the colour and texture of the hair had to be relevant to the expected climatic conditions their product would be living in. The sample of humans that they were preparing to occupy this planet would not develop the skills to travel from their immediate surroundings for many millennia in the future. Simon and Loraine were astounded when it dawned on them what this symposium meant and its importance to the future of the human race. It was obvious that the community were of a superior race to the humanoids they were engineering. The group recognised the presence of the newcomers. Their attention to the visitors brought their proceedings to a halt and their leader requested the strangers not to depart.

"Do not be alarmed, please stay and communicate with us."

"We are able to understand your telepathy and will willingly stay and share our knowledge and experience."

"We have been observing this planet's evolution and believe that it has now reached a point at which it can sustain humanoid life forms, capable of self-motivation and progression. So far, to our dismay, the life that exists has survived rather well but without any motivation for advancement."

"Is it that you have made it too easy for them to survive?"

"We have the responsibility to provide the means to enable our creatures to overcome the difficulties that Nature will force upon them. We have no desire to allow them to perish, before they have the opportunity to advance."

"It is our opinion that existence itself is a paradox. The main strength in humanity is its inherent weakness."

"How can this be? Is it really logical to say that inability to survive could be an asset?"

"Many species of animals and insects are able to survive without having to progress to a new level of development and are plentifully populating the planet. To change the balance of nature you have to produce a need. If you are aiming to create a human race with self-motivation for progress then you have to ensure that they need to progress in order to survive."

"We can accept the wisdom of your argument and will consider introducing need into our scheme".

"What is the purpose of your undertaking and how is it of benefit to your own society?"

"We owe our own existence to such a visitation from others many millions of years ago. Now we have developed to the level of ability which enables us to similarly assist the development of others. The presence of you two at this event presents a problem which we must resolve. Are you members of the population of this planet?"

"Indeed, we belong to the human race and we are not aware of any human or other beings departing from or arriving on this earth in any physical form at any time in the earth's history."

"Your presence here is an enigma and challenges all our expectations. The form of humanity that we are genetically engineering is not designed to possess the capability to develop into beings like yourselves."

Simon, ignoring this interesting comment continued,

"We were puzzled by observing a craft unlike any we have seen, that was travelling over the mountain without making contact with the ground."

"What you saw was an adaptation of our normal land craft. It has the ability to compensate for the primary *force which holds everything close to your planet and can therefore leave its surface."*

"We have no knowledge of this Primary Force and wish to learn more."

"Your planet was initially formed by a spinning mass that accumulated matter to form a large enough body to stay together. The force between this mass, and other parts of the Universe is called 'gravitation'. The attraction caused by this force brought together into this mass, particles of material necessary to sustain life as you know it."

"This appears to be a very fundamental force that we do not yet understand."

"It is the dominant force that helped create the universe in its present state and will maintain it well in to the future."

"How did you overcome this dominant force to enable your transporter to perform as we saw it?"

"Nothing that we know of can totally overcome the effect of gravitational force but we can find ways to nullify its effect on a particular body to a degree. This is similar to spinning a flat stone over the surface of water. While skimming it will defy the influence of gravity rather better than one not spinning and so will travel further over the water before surrendering to the force."

"Are you able to see the results of your efforts in the future?"

"We are able to assess the possibilities available in the future, but to actually observe the future is beyond our ability or desire."

"We can accept the sense in that. Does it indicate that you are of our past and we are of your future?"

"You have stated the only plausible explanation, however

we have no proof. If you could describe what, in your era, you see of our city and citadel, which we named, Atlantis, we may be able to judge the possible time lapse between us."

"If we were to divulge this information we would be giving you a window into the future. You have just told us that you do not desire such knowledge."

"If the two of you are a product of our process, we shall forever be proud of our intervention."

"We believe that this intrusion into this day of your lives is an incident for us to cherish privately and not to share with others at random. Perhaps by tomorrow we shall consider it all a figment of our imagination or a wild dream that we will hold to ourselves until we feel it judicious to share the experience with others."

With that the link was broken, and the vision faded with the rising sun. Slowly Simon and Loraine drifted apart and sank exhausted to their beds, he on his bedroll outside the Princess's door and she to her lonely cabin aboard the Bella Doria.

NINETEEN

BACK TO NORMAL

On the third day after their arrival at St Hilarion, Simon was woken by the most precious person in his life. Loraine informed him that Limassol Castle was visible from the Bella Doria and King Richard's fleet was aligning in the bay for an invasion landing. Simon picked up his bedroll, from outside the Princess's room and knocked on her door. He expected to be waiting some time as he knew that the Princess and her new lady-in-waiting dressed lightly at night due to the high temperatures at that time of year. He had no wish to embarrass the young ladies despite the importance of the news.

Anxious not to disclose the source of his information, he disguised the news as gossip overheard from guards discussing a message received by pigeon from Limassol Castle. The Princess's joy was beyond description at the thought that she would soon see Richard again.

King Isaac summoned his three 'guests' to his presence before lunch-time. Apparently a messenger pigeon had actually arrived by then, with news of an invasion. Looking accusingly at all three of them, he demanded to be informed of the military and maritime strength of

Richard Coeur de Lion. When he received no response, he threatened them with evil malice.

"We can assure your Highness of our complete ignorance of the information you are seeking. None of us has had the honour of recent acquaintance with King Richard let alone have any knowledge of his fleet or army. All we do understand, you already know, that he was on his way to do battle in the Holy Land".

Are you aware that he captured Limassol castle?"

Simon, feeling confident in the flow of events, challenged the king,

"Did he, in fact, capture it or take possession of it, Sire?"

"What, pray, is the difference?"

Simon, now skilfully goaded the arrogant king,

"If he has actually captured the castle, then he must have used a very large army and overcome its defenders to do so. But if he has just taken possession of it, then this would suggest collusion from within or a simple surrender to a vastly superior force in order to avoid bloody combat.

How long did it take for King Richard to achieve this, Your Highness?"

Isaac, not at all happy that Simon had taken control of the discourse, which was not progressing in the manner he had planned, appeared confused and angry. "Apparently all this happened this very morning."

"Then that would indicate a very short battle, or indeed no combat at all and either way confirms Richard's reputation as a formidable foe."

The furious king, at a loss for an answer, dismissed the three to their respective quarters and ordered them to remain there until further notice. Happy to be away from him they found it difficult to hide their elation at the news they had heard.

By then Richard's progress was the only talking point throughout the island. He had accurately assessed the strength of the opposition to be negligible and had left instructions for his navy to proceed to the Holy Land along with a major part of his land forces. He was successful in this only because of Isaac's deep unpopularity and his armed men had deserted him in droves and joined Richard's cause, to rescue his Princess. As he travelled across the land, country folk laid down their tasks and followed him anxious to aid Richard in raising their yoke of oppression and liberating Cyprus from the grip of Isaac.

Richard had little time even for food as city and castle surrendered without a fight. He was universally perceived as rescuer rather than conqueror.

Isaac, unable to accept the turn of events, was highly disturbed, and as such was unpredictable and very dangerous. When Richard's forces reached Hilarion and camped in the jousting grounds below the barbican, Isaac watched helpless as his castle guards abandoned their defensive posts and joined Richard's forces, irreparably damaging the entrance gates and portcullis, in their defiance.

In an act of blind rage, Isaac gathered the remaining three of his personal bodyguards and marched towards Princess Berengaria's quarters. Simon had anticipated this possibility and had warned the ladies to stay behind the strong, locked door and not to open to anyone but himself or King Richard.

Meanwhile he waited in the arched low passage that offered the only access to the room. He had a shield, acquired from one of the fleeing soldiers secured to his left forearm and his sword in his right hand, ready-drawn. He felt that the numerical superiority of his adversaries would not amount to much, as in the narrow passage not more than two could attack him at one time and in the confined space would be more likely to impede each other than endanger him.

"You bar our path at your peril, Sir Simon", the King, who was leading the party at that point, shouted from the far end of the passage.

"I foresee no peril to myself or to my Wards, Your Highness. On the other hand, you have chosen a path towards misfortune and defeat."

"I shall defend my realm as I choose. If I hold a dagger to the throat of Richard's future Queen, he will not dare to come near me."

"As ever, you are thinking like a lowly brigand instead of rising to your station. You have no possible access to the Princess, and should you even attempt to carry out your threat her hundred Basque Navarre archers in King Richard's army would cut you to shreds with their arrows before you could complete your sentence."

Looking directly at the guards, he continued,

"My personal recommendation, to anyone who does not wish to be cut down by my sword for supporting a misplaced cause, is to leave now and join King Richard's army, by way of asking for his pardon."

The two mercenaries who had been pushed in front of Isaac Comnenus, momentarily looked behind them for a means of escape, but Isaac edged them forward, bringing them within Simon's sword stroke. Simon restrained himself from an easy lunge and simply prepared his shield. The attackers, thinking that Simon's act was a defensive gesture, both lifted their swords for a strike from above, a posture de falcone, and left themselves unprotected. It was easy for Simon to parry the simultaneous strike of the two swords with a slight swing of his shield. He then inflicted considerable damage to the sword-carrying arms whilst they were still held above, and blocked from coming down by the shield. The two dropped their weapons, which clattered to the ground at Simon's feet, turned, and pushing past the King, fled. The third guard joined them without a word, leaving the King deserted and extremely vulnerable.

However, the victor could then afford to appear magnanimous. "Perhaps it would be better for you if we could forget this incident and go welcome King Richard and escort his future Queen to him together, Sire". Isaac, who was holding only a dagger in his hand, snatched up an abandoned sword to surrender to King Richard, and grudgingly accepted defeat.

Hilarion had fallen!

The two ladies, who had readied themselves for this occasion, led the way and were followed by the two men. They passed through the now empty passageways, out on to the open stairs and down the mountain-side to reach the wide open and destroyed portcullis, where a group of Richard's nobles were waiting to escort them to the King. Apparently, their arrival was expected, thanks to the reports from the fleeing guards, and cheers rang out from all ranks. Everyone was happy that again, no blood had been shed that day.

In the evening Richard surprised his followers by inviting Isaac to dine with him and his company. The rest of the army were given leave to merry-make in their camp and long before midnight many tired and inebriated soldiers had fallen into the comfort of a deep sleep. Eventually, Richard dismissed some of his commanders to their beds but kept Simon beside him and then turned to Isaac.

"Well, Sir Isaac, what are we to do with you, now that you have no kingdom to rule? From what I have been told, the punishment that you deserve is harsh indeed."

"Sire, I humbly crave your pardon. I pledge to you my life's loyalty and beg of you your Christian charity."

"Sir, my charity is spent on this, your final meal in noble company. You shall be banished from this island that you seized and ruled ignobly. Before dawn you shall board a vessel that will sail west for two whole days and there in the middle of the ocean you will be transferred to a small boat with only an amount of bread and water. This should afford you adequate time to reflect on your crimes and repent of your sins. You will be in God's hands and in charge of your own destiny."

With that the King dismissed Isaac into the secure charge of the guards.

The King then turned to Simon. "Sir Simon, we are very much in your debt. I can offer you land and a position in my army or navy. It is for you to decide."

"Your Highness, I have done no more than carry out the responsibilities entrusted to me by your friend

King Philip and Queen Joan, your sister. My reward has already been granted in the successful completion of my appointed task."

"Your reputation for modesty has preceded you. I have now taken this island but after I marry Princess Berengaria in Limassol Castle next Sunday I will have no further use for this land. I am offering it to you with my protection, if you accept my flag."

"Sire, your generosity exceeds all bounds. As to my future, destiny demands I follow another path and the sale of this island would substantially add to your war chest."

Richard much enamoured with that thought then contemplated possible purchasers at a time when all the royal houses and the Church were concentrating their resources on the Crusade.

However, at this point Signor Marcos, the old Knights Templar who had joined Richard's party in Limassol, attracted the King's attention. "You Highness, I may be of assistance. My Order has been searching for land for a while now. If I were to inform our Grand Master of this situation I am certain he would consider the matter favourably."

The King, satisfied that his predicament may be solved, thanked the Templar for his consideration and gave his permission to approach the Grand Master. Again, he thanked Simon as his introduction to the Templar could prove invaluable. As they retired for the night he added to Simon enigmatically, "Before you go, remember that turning down any further token of our generosity could offend us."

Loraine, who had been at his side throughout,

squeezed his hand to warn him to take care in his reply but he merely gripped her hand more tightly with the ambiguous words,

"We thank you for everything, my Lord."

TWENTY

THE HOLY LAND

The morning after the royal wedding and subsequent revelling, Simon and Loraine arrived back to the Bella Doria at dawn. The night-watchman acknowledged them as Simon left Loraine in her cabin and returned to his navigator's room. The sun was just beginning to clear the horizon, so the cabin was still near darkness and he rolled on to his hammock, having stumbled over a large wooden chest that had been left near his bed.

The next thing he knew, he was being woken by a seaman, with a request from the Admiral that he join him for lunch. After Simon's time away from the ship, the friends enjoyed sharing tales of their recent experiences. They agreed that although they would miss her presence the departure of the Princess would ease the overcrowding of the ship. The stores had been replenished to their full capacity for their on-going journey as although it was a relatively short distance to the Holy Land, they were not certain of availability in a battle area and would certainly have to pay inflated prices.

The Admiral then mentioned the 'special' delivery that had been made for Simon the previous evening. A sealed envelope and a chest had been placed in his cabin by a military escort of King Richard's men, suggesting that the contents were of great value.

Quite embarrassed by the rare honour, Simon explained, "I did promise not to decline the King's next act of generosity, so I guess he took advantage of me". Anxious to put his friend at ease the Admiral offered words of wisdom. "My friend, your personal attributes are immeasurable, but for a person of your standing, who may be considering matrimony shortly to a young lady of high social status, you do happen to be rather short of worldly assets. You must also consider your very loyal friends. At the moment they are earning their passage by work on board. However, at the end of this venture, unless you agree to serve one King or another and accept their patronage, you will encounter many difficulties."

Simon, who acknowledged that he had little experience in taking responsibility for others, sought the Admiral's advice.

"Your seamanship is beyond compare and your intuition would make you an excellent trader. As to your men, they have proved themselves under the most demanding circumstances. However, whilst you personally have been involved in this Crusade, as much as anyone else, my belief is that it has never been your battle or a situation of your choice.

As for myself, I shall benefit enormously financially. I could double my trading fleet if I could find the right person to accept a partnership. I would gladly give you this ship if you agreed to sail it as captain in partnership with me and my family."

Simon was impressed by his friend's insight and generous offer and agreed that his involvement in the Crusade was entirely circumstantial. "I cannot kill for gain or for an ideal. I fear this Crusade is not as it is represented. All religions preach a lesson of peace and harmony between men regardless of their differences. They teach tolerance not confrontation and yet they do not live by these principles. The Crusade is promoted by the wealthy for their personal gain and as always will be at the expense of others already less fortunate. My own involvement will always be to attempt to minimize the personal cost to both sides which I will do to the best of my ability. On the other matter, your generous offer is beyond the bounds of friendship. I appreciate the gesture with all my heart, but that cannot be my future. I will however gladly accept guidance on the means of sharing King Richard's gift with my comrades."

The Admiral was happy to be of help. It was estimated that the chest contained about fifteen thousand gold coins, for Simon, an inconceivable fortune but the Admiral was pragmatic.

"This amounts to a very worthy sum which you have earned deservedly. I guess much of it came to King Richard as a result of the defeat of Isaac Comnenus, when his treasure would have been sequestered. As you were instrumental in that evil man's overthrow, the gift can be considered your share of the booty."

But Simon, still overwhelmed by the enormity of the wealth asked, "How shall I divide it between my men, for I can only carry a small part of it safely on my person?"

"One hundred pieces of gold would make any bearer a

wealthy person. As to the actual weight of wealth, why do you think Queen Joan has Signor Marcos, the Templar, in her retinue?"

He went on to explain that while the Queen travelled with a small number of valuables for her immediate use, her main treasure was held by the Templars and so she kept their representative near her. Simon was surprised to hear that, like Queen Joan, many other royal and wealthy families deposited the bulk of their treasuries with the Templars to be held in their vaults on the Island of Sicily. They would be given a signed and sealed receipt and guarantee, to be used to the value of their goods.

At first Simon could not see how this arrangement could help him and his friends but the Admiral added,

"The Templars have access to negotiable assets in all the main cities even in the Islamic world. An authorised note of credit from a Templar can be readily converted to the local currency. This avoids the inconvenience of carrying bulky coins and the risk of loss. You, Simon, can hand over any amount of your treasure to your friend, the Templar, and in exchange he will provide you with a document, to its value, which you can carry easily and safely".

Simon, who knew nothing of this, was eager to learn how the system worked and how it could benefit the Templars.

"Many people in trade need capital which they may not have at the time they require it. They might be willing to pay a premium to have credit made available to them. The Templars provide this service. By using the deposits that have been made with them they can provide loans for which they charge interest until full repayment has been made. These transactions provide the Templars with the opportunity to add substantially to their already considerable wealth."

Simon naïvely remarked,

"That appears to be an easy way of accumulating wealth."

"May be, but it is also rather risky. The possessor of wealth is always the target for envy and enmity. The accumulation of wealth brings with it power of a kind that even royalty may find uncomfortable to live with. Also there are occasions when the borrowers do not find it easy to pay back the loans or chose not to. It can be a complicated way to make a living."

"While this could never be a chosen life style for me, I concede that it could be a very valuable service for many and we could most definitely benefit from it in our present situation."

At this point Lady Loraine entered the cabin and cheerfully responded to the greetings from both men.

"What matter can be so important that it detains the two of you in this stuffy cabin on such a wonderful day?"

"King Richard's generous present has given me a number of not unpleasant problems, which I was endeavouring to overcome with our very knowledgeable friend, here. We have already solved the problem of my parting company with the loyal friends that have stayed by me for so long. The Admiral will keep them on board, as crew for the journey, and I shall be rewarding them with enough gold to provide them each with an independent life back in their own countries. We will then remove from the chest enough for our own immediate future and deposit the rest of the gold with the Templars for future access by us".

It was when Simon admitted that his only remaining concern was his lack of experience at handling every day affairs, and any money they should have to carry with them, that Loraine laughed, "That is why you have me, Simon. My mother once ingeniously prepared a coat for my father with two hundred gold coins sewn into the lining. Most women are born with the ability to cope with such matters."

"Then we have no other problem than to get married."

"Is my Sir Simon proposing marriage in front of a witness?"

Simon moved close to Loraine and dropping on to one knee took both her hands in his, "Would My Lady consent to join her humble servant in matrimony?"

"Yes, I most certainly will! Are there any other questions?"

Simon kissed both the hands he was holding, before rising to his feet and enquiring "When and where?"

This led to some debate as they remembered that King Philip and his Queen wished to be present at Simon's wedding and also that King Richard and Berengaria, on their way to a second wedding reception in Acre may also like to share their special day. On the other hand it was possible for them to marry immediately as both the Padre and the Admiral were qualified to perform the ceremony.

It was the Admiral that broke in to be the first to congratulate the pair, "I think we should first inform Queen Joan and then all others on board and then celebrate the occasion with a bottle of my best wine."

Two days later they disembarked in Acre to an enthusiastic greeting from King Philip and his Queen. Their arrival was a happy distraction from the other events around them. When Simon asked the King's permission for the Lady Loraine's hand in marriage, Philip not only gave his blessing but offered to carry out the ceremony himself.

"You will honour us beyond all else by performing the ceremony my Lord but we would be pleased to make it a rather private one as we do not wish to divert attention from the other important matters of the day."

Although the couple wished for a quiet affair, Richard and Berengaria insisted on being present and it was, in the event, a very splendid occasion.

After their wedding they were accommodated in a tent not far from the French Royals, who had desired to have them close. They were in an encampment that surrounded the besieged city of Acre. Their position was highly vulnerable and dangerous as the city had been under siege for nearly two years and the inhabitants were becoming desperate. Saladin's forces were making every effort to break through the French and English lines to get provisions and reinforcements through to relieve the beleaguered city.

Unlike Richard, who was known to favour personal combat, Philip preferred long range warfare and particularly the use of the siege machine, which he was reputed to have designed. The gigantic catapult had to be manufactured by the blacksmiths and carpenters on the spot that the King indicated, as it was so large it had very limited mobility. He had spent many hours supervising the construction of the huge machine. Understanding its potential power, the Muslims had launched many skirmishes in attempts to prevent its completion. It was during one of these sorties that King Philip was injured by a Saracen arrow that had pierced his chainmail between his neck and left shoulder. Due to the urgent work he was undertaking at the time, the king delayed treatment, exacerbating an already inflamed wound. Eventually he went to his physicians who spent a considerable time tending him.

The following day the King was clearly worse and Simon, privately, offered to assist him. But the King waived him aside saying that his Royal Physicians were able to deal with the situation and he preferred that Simon help him with the fighting. In spite of his friendship and loyalty to the King, Simon was true to his conscience and replied,

"My Lord, I am not the only one questioning the justification and holiness of this venture, which you have embarked on. I do believe that as a great King your responsibility is with your people in France, to guide them, under your leadership to unite as one nation. The land you inherited is your birth right and all the peoples of France should owe their allegiance to one King, who in turn gives his devotion and loyalty to his people."

But Philip challenged this concept of right and duty, "What of the Holy Land being ruled by Saladin?"

"Every tiny part of this earth or universe is holy. It has been created by the same god and for the same reason. Saladin is the presiding King of this land and he has never been known to maltreat or murder a Christian for simply being different. He rules over all his people without discrimination or prejudice. The followers of Moses have no complaint, nor does most of the Levant or other Christian Churches."

King Philip looked across to the Knights Templar, "How do the Templars view this situation?"

"Our Order exists in many lands with the consent of their rulers. We can only accomplish this by respecting the rule of the land. We certainly have establishments in the lands of Islam without encountering harassment or prejudice.

With that the King, who was obviously still in considerable pain, assured them that he would keep their discussions in mind, wished them goodnight and retired to bed.

The arrival of King Richard and his massive fleet at Acre had strengthened the will and vigour of the siege armies, surrounding the city. Just one month later, to Saladin's anger and against his orders, the prevention of reinforcements to the defenders finally led to surrender. However, disappointed as he was at the loss of his city, Saladin's respect for human values led to the signing of a treaty, that would return the true Cross to the Roman Church and facilitate the exchange of prisoners.

Later that same morning Philip summoned Simon to the Great Tent that was the gathering place for the Kings and those of high office. Many heated arguments had taken place in the tent throughout the day but all was calm when Simon and Loraine arrived. King Philip was still in grave discomfort from his shoulder wound and was reclining on a couch that had been brought in for his comfort.

King Richard and Queen Berengaria were about to leave

but welcomed the newly-wed couple warmly. Richard's broadsword was leaning against his throne without its scabbard but as he left he glanced at it remarking, "I shall have no need of you for the rest of the day, old friend."

King Philip and his Queen were left alone in the tent with Simon and Loraine.

"Simon, my Queen and I have decided that our task in this war in completed. We shall depart for France as soon as my health allows. We very much wish that the two of you would join us."

Simon, without replying to the King, approached him and reached out towards his damaged shoulder with his right hand. The others noticed the appearance of a glow between the two bodies. Although physical contact was not made, Simon felt disorientated by the experience and leaned out for support, as he felt in danger of falling. As he swayed forwards he touched the sword that Richard had left behind. He immediately moved his hand but as the others watched the highly polished blade turned dull momentarily before returning to its original shine. Seeing his friend's unsteady move, Philip rose from his couch instinctively to assist Simon to his feet. The Queen was the first to recognise the impossibility of this act and rushed to help the King back to his resting position. The King raised his hand to allay her fears and gradually gaining in strength made his own way back to his couch.

The Queen turned to Simon and Loraine for an explanation of what she had just witnessed.

"My Lady, I used my body as a vehicle to direct the bad humours and damaging influences away from the King. I have already passed most of this corruption to Mother

Earth, where there is endless capacity. I will rid my body of all the evil but the process leaves me weak and I will need to recuperate".

"How is this possible, are you a magician?"

"I am not aware of any magical abilities Your Highness but we all have ways of easing the hurt of others. By a warm smile or a kiss we are sharing the burden that ails them. The healing ways of nature have been with us from the beginning of time. Maybe if we all learned to accept this and lived in harmony with it we may have a longer and more fulfilling life."

"We are indebted to you. How can we repay your selflessness?"

"The only thing I would ask is that no-one mentions these accomplishments to anyone. I could never be able to offer this service to all that need it. You can imagine the burden this would put me under, with the many casualties of war. I believe the Church would see me as a heretic and burn me at the stake".

"You have our sympathy, without question, Sir Simon. We shall disguise my improvement for a time and later praise our physicians for their excellent work and duly recompense them. However, Simon, you must allow me some way of repaying this act of kindness."

"Your Highness, it was through you that I met Loraine and so you have given me the greatest gift of my life. You gave your blessing for our marriage and we shall forever be grateful for your counsel and your friendship. The only one request we have now is your permission to take our leave of your company. We believe it is time for us to part."

"Simon, we feel that you and Loraine are part of our family. We shall find it difficult not to have you near us."

"We are honoured, Your Majesty, but you will soon be departing for France, where many situations will be requiring your undivided attention. However, I am certain that King Richard would be very grateful if you were to offer to accompany his Queen Berengaria to France. I believe Richard may be feeling rather inhibited by her presence in these dangerous times.

As for us, our destiny will be guiding us in a different direction, to new horizons. We shall cherish our memories of you and all our friends."

King Philip then surprised both Simon and Loraine with a most perceptive and obscure remark, "We have been aware of changes to Queen Berengaria. In spite of the circumstances she appears very relaxed and content with her position in life."

"Was that not expected, My Lord?"

"May be not, but all is well and she is in good health and very happy."

Just on that Richard reappeared in the tent to join their final farewell.

Simon and Loraine then left hand in hand and walked out of one life into another.

TWENTY-ONE

GARDEN OF TRANQUILITY

Just after noon on the day of their departure, Simon, who was now again calling himself Salem, and Loraine, who had taken an Arabic name, Zahra, slipped from their tent on the vast encampment for the last time. They had hidden their western clothes under long, hooded cloaks and made first for the small market-place. Here they carefully selected clothes suitable for their long, hot journey, and provisions to support them on their way. Then Salem, under the watchful eye of Zahra, bartered for three healthy camels. They left town taking a road to the north hoping to meet a caravan travelling in the direction of Damascus. The roads leading away from Acre were crowded with travellers desperate to escape the horrors of war and the aftermath of the siege. Defenders of the city feared a fate like those of Jerusalem some years earlier that had been put to the sword by the conquering Crusaders.

Before long the young travellers had joined one of the many camel trains that were fleeing the troubled city.

They spent the night in a tent erected at the edge of the caravan and before surrendering to a much needed sleep, they informed Sinbad and Bathsheba that they were, at last, on their way home to Basra.

After early morning prayers and a short breakfast they all prepared their camels and the small number of horses for the journey. Fellow travellers helped each other with the preparations and no assistance was declined. This soon led to an increase in expertise and camaraderie among the group. The Caravan Master strode along the line checking the efficiency of the preparations and constantly repeating his dire warning that the desert was "out there, waiting to swallow the casual or careless traveller into its ample and hungry gut". However, being immediately aware of their higher status, he directed Salem and Zahra to the very front of the procession to ensure that they did not get lost.

While the land soon became wild and rocky scrub, the real desert was still some distance away, and this gradual approach enabled Zahra to wonder at the extra-ordinary sights around her, that she could never have imagined in her earlier life.

It was early in the morning of their third day of travelling when Salem was helping Zahra on to her camel, she gripped his sleeve to attract his attention. "I feel we are being watched".

Not fully appreciating her concern, he replied, playfully, "The whole caravan is watching us, my love."

"That is not what is disturbing me. I am sensing an aggressive force watching us from behind the rise of those dunes to the left of us."

"Hold on to my hand and we shall investigate together."

As the rest of the caravan was ready to depart, Salem raised a hand in warning to the Caravan Master. By the time he reached them everyone was aware of the problem. It was a renegade troop of crusaders who had decided that it was a profitable escapade to deprive travellers of their valuables. Salem described the imminent danger to the master just as the raiders appeared from behind the distant dune. The rest of the travellers were alerted to the approaching threat, and began to panic in fear of an attack. Salem indicated to them to keep silent and still as statues. Fear froze the entire caravan to a tableau.

The horse-riding bandits continued their approach at speed but passed the caravan without a side-long glance and galloped on towards an unseen prey, disappearing from view in a rising cloud of sand, to the speechless amazement of the travellers. The spell broke and everyone cheered in relief and proceeded hurriedly to leave the area. To the bewildered Master and the nearby passengers Salem merely remarked, "An irresponsible band on an irrational venture"! But he gave no further explanation of the phenomenal event. In fact with combined powerful energy, the two had created an illusion of their caravan to be seen five hundred paces ahead of them to the north-east. This mirage would keep the same distance from the raiders and taunt them until they fell exhausted and lost. Meanwhile the real caravan had been hidden from their view in a heat haze.

That night was to prove one of the most magical of their lives and although they did not recognise it until later, it was to change their lives for ever. They had reached a lush oasis in the early afternoon and had settled for the night in the shade of a large date palm.

The caravan master had informed all the gathering

that everything in the desert had its owner. If they found dates on the ground they could take and eat them, but if they picked them from the palms it would be stealing and the owner of the trees could punish the offender as he wished.

After all had chosen their resting places, the water vessels had been filled, and the women had completed their chores. Then, with the agreement of their menfolk, they draped blankets between the tents to afford them some privacy, and bathed in the lake, luxuriating in its cooling waters and ridding themselves of the desert sand.

As Zahra stepped out of the water, she discarded the towel which she had wrapped round her head like a turban and dragged it behind her leaving a trail in the sand. While she had bathed, Salem had sat by their tent idly playing his flute, lost in wonder at the glory of nature around him. As Zahra approached him her long, loose hair glowing, the colour of burnished copper in the setting sun, his heart burst with desire for his beautiful wife, and he knew that she was reading his thoughts and was at one with them.

His music then was in his soul and for that instant they heard no sound, the earth stood still and they had eyes for none but each other.

Later, as the night's darkness pushed the last of the daylight into the history of the day, the star clusters, in profusion beyond imagination, lit the sky with a new light and a crescent new moon hung like a pendant in the void, they lay entranced entwined as one. The night sounds were disturbed only by the gently strains from a nearby tent, as a lone traveller, moved by the aura of the night, sang hauntingly of the ache in his heart for his distant love.

But as day followed night, the dawn light broke the spell. Putting behind them the enchantment, they were all soon busily about the business of the day.

The rest of their journey to Damascus, the oldest city in the world, was without incident. Once there, they separated from the caravan and proceeded alone to the shores of the mighty Euphrates.

They followed the west bank of the river down-steam crossing to the east by the precarious raft ferry. With the River Tigris ahead of them it seemed a short distance to home. They finally reached the great city of Baghdad, which Salem explained to Zahra meant 'City of Harmony'. At the city gates they met an unexpected welcome party and were overjoyed to see the jubilant figure of Sinbad, with a lively band of his sailors, waiting for them. Sinbad immediately took over arrangements by sending off two of his companions to find a buyer for the fine camels. Both Zahra and Salem were sad at parting from the animals that had been well-behaved and faithful companions on their journey. Zahra approached the camels and stroked their foreheads and the animals tossed their heads and snorted their appreciation. Sinbad then offered the travellers two bags made of goatskin, for their valued belongings and suggested that any unwanted trifles be given away to by-passers as they would find anything they wished for in the busy markets.

Anxious as they were to be on their way, this was not to be as Sinbad's presence had not gone unnoticed. As they were preparing to dine and rest at the caravanserai, on their first night in Baghdad, a messenger arrived from the Caliph with an invitation for the family to attend him at the Palace. Although Sinbad was already familiar with the splendour, the magnificence of the Caliph's Palace took the others by surprise. Zahra, who was acquainted with many noble houses, palaces and castles throughout Europe, was most impressed. The architecture, that defied all suggestion of a fortress, aspired to the very heights of elegance and exquisiteness. The structure had few straight lines but many smooth curves and domes and gentle, decorative towers, with balconies around them instead of battlements. The blend of pastel colours in the sunset painted a scene in harmony with nature. Zahra felt the tears spring to her eyes as she was overcome by the awe-inspiring beauty of it all. She tightened her grip on Salem's hand to keep her hold on reality as they entered the palace.

It was like drifting through a magical world and she felt no song or poetry could be as beautiful as the scenes she was witnessing as they were guided through a multitude of wide passages and hallways towards the Caliph's presence.

The Caliph, seated cross-legged on his sadir, greeted them informally in a friendly and easy manner. Zahra found the Caliph's seat most unusual in its design and unlike any she had seen. It was waist-high and long enough for a person to recline full length, opulently ornate, with many silken cushions for complete comfort and relaxation.

The Caliph sat resplendent in a magnificent layered garment, the product of highly skilled tailors.

Guided by their escort they halted and then, following him, took a step closer to His highness and his lady seated next to him, and bowed in respect. The Caliph signalled Sinbad to a cushion on his right and his company to seats nearby. It was obvious that the Caliph was seeking news of affairs abroad as he opened the discourse with a query to Sinbad,

"What news of the naval force that you have been preparing for our Caliphate? Is it ready to assist Sultan Saladin's efforts to defend our faith and traditions against the aggression of the Christians?"

At that moment and before Sinbad could answer, the Caliph's wife rose and offered to show Zahra the rest of the Palace and they walked off holding hands like old friends, leaving the men to solve the problems of the world.

"My Beloved Ruler", began Sinbad, "the only waters accessible to your realm are the Persian Gulf and the Indian Ocean. We already have a very adequate fleet at your command, capable of handling any eventuality in those areas. However, all the enemy Christian forces are in the Mediterranean Sea."

"Can we not sail our fleet to the Mediterranean Sea to engage the enemy?"

"Until recently that would have been deemed impossible, but my son tells me that this can now be accomplished. He has circumnavigated the African continent on his journeys in the last twenty-six months."

"Sinbad, you must be jesting! What naval force could be expected to travel for so long a time and still be prepared to engage the enemy at the end of it?"

At this point Salem intervened to explain further.

"My Caliph, Protector of the faith, the journey and adventure that took two years of my life enhanced and enriched me beyond measure. However, the voyage of a fleet could take as little as two months, but even this would not be easy logistically. In my opinion such an effort would be costly and unnecessary. The Christian forces have now reached the pinnacle of their strength. Their ability to wage war is now subsiding. King Philip of France has returned home with his forces. The King of Austria is in dispute with King Richard the Lion Heart and there are others who may be in sympathy with him."

The Caliph was impressed with Salem's knowledge and understanding of the situation and asked advice on how he should most advantageously proceed.

"My Caliph, if, as I anticipate, Sultan Saladin is successful in this conflict, he could become either a powerful ally or a dangerous antagonist. If we ensure that he gets all the support and assistance he requires from the Caliphate then we shall be a party to his victory. This will ensure his allegiance to the Protector of the Faith."

At this, the Caliph sought to appoint Salem as commander of all such strategies to assist the Sultan. But Salem replied,

"My Lord, you honour me with such high office, but I have journeyed long and have not seen my mother for more than two years and plan to introduce to her my beloved wife. If you are of the same mind, I can return in a short while, but in the meantime I am certain that someone in your service can fulfil the role. The integrity and diligence of your Vezir-i-azam, Grand Vizier, for example, is well known."

"I am afraid that such an appointment could cause a problem for the Sultan Saladin. He may feel his position, in the field of action, compromised by the presence of a person of such high status as my Grand Vizier."

"That, of course, is a possibility, but if the Vizier subjects himself to the Sultan's absolute command and offers him his unquestioned loyalty from the beginning, this should ensure harmony between the two authorities."

"This proposition I shall consider overnight. Now I believe it is time to dine."

Father and son followed the caliph out of his Court Room and into an adjacent private dining room, which served only the Sovereign and his family members. The two ladies soon joined the men, who were already seated on the ample cushions arranged around a magnificent mosaic dining tray which was heavily laden with delicious and exotic foods.

When the servants had withdrawn and the company was private, the Caliph's wife astounded the gathering by announcing to all, that she knew Zahra to be expecting twins, a boy and a girl and added that she must now take great care.

Sinbad and Salem looked to each other and then both turned to Zahra in amazement, searching for confirmation. When they realised that Zahra was as astonished as the rest of them, the Caliph came to the rescue, explaining that his wife had the gift of seeing such things and was never wrong and they would do well to heed her advice. The Caliph added jovially,

"This is very good news for you Salem but I see it definitely rules you out of contention for command of the forces to be sent to Saladin."

Salem reached out to take Zahra's hand overwhelmed with his love for her and excitement for their future.

The rest of the evening was spent in the most congenial

manner, with good food and excellent company. Zahra declined the offer of a sedan chair when they finally bade farewell, vowing loyalty and friendship, as they parted company at the end of a very delightful and unexpectedly exciting evening.

Back in their room at the caravanserai they lay wondering again at the news they had been given. Sharing their happy memories of their recent journey they had no doubt of the time their twins were conceived and they saw again the crescent moon and heard again the haunting sound of the plaintive love song on the air.

At the breakfast table the following morning Salem told his father of his financial involvement with the Knights Templars, and their banking facilities. Sinbad, unfamiliar with the system advised putting it to the test and withdrawing the wealth and taking it with them to Basra and to the safety of their family home.

Salem and Zahra could find no reason to object and while Zahra was easily persuaded to be escorted to the bazaar by a couple of Sinbad's sailors, Sinbad and Salem took the rest of the sailors, for security, with them to the clearing house address in Baghdad, which was listed on the document provided for them by Signor Marcos.

Following directions given to them by the master of the caravanserai, the group arrived at a residence in the centre of the city's residential area. The house was surrounded by a high wall and could be entered only by a very solid-looking closed door. A sharp rap on the polished brass knocker brought a swift response. A neatly dressed man of tall stature, and of unreadable age, appeared at the door and inquired into the reason for their call. Salem handed the servant, the documents from Signor Marcos and the letter they had been busy preparing over breakfast. Glancing at the paperwork the servant opened the door wider and invited Sinbad and Salem to follow him through the courtyard towards the house, while suggesting that the rest of the party should relax in the garden under the grape-vine trellis where someone would attend to them shortly. Sinbad indicated his agreement and then followed Salem along a well-paved path towards the entrance to the house.

Four gardeners, busy at their tasks, acknowledged the greeting from the sailors and continued with their work.

The visitors found the place to have a pleasing atmosphere. The inside was comfortably appointed but with no trace of opulence. A heavy door opened to reveal a large entrance hall, floored with white marble partially covered with an assortment of small carpets. In the middle of the hall the marble floor appeared to be rising seamlessly into a flower-shaped fountain. Each petal of this marble flower was ejecting a water jet that arched gently to collide in the centre of the flower before being drawn back into the depths of the fountain.

Sinbad and Salem were shown to comfortable seats while the documents were being studied. As they waited, Salem searched through the rooms with his thoughts and Sinbad watched as his son gradually drifted away. One particular room resisted Salem's insistent probing, but on his perseverance he was eventually permitted to enter. Inside he observed a very old gentleman seated on a divan near a large window that overlooked the garden and afforded wonderful views to the west.

"Salem el Sinbad, it is good to see you in person. You are a most welcome visitor to my humble abode."

Salem thoroughly shocked that the gentleman should take the initiative in their communication immediately broke off the contact while he regained his composure. His self-isolation had lasted long enough for him not to notice the return of the servant who was requesting them to follow him to an inner office. Sinbad was nudging him to attract his attention. A clerk, seated on a cushion behind a low table had placed the two documents folded as if their task was done.

"Gentlemen, your transaction can be completed immediately; the adjustment on your credit is an extra sum of seventy-five gold units."

"That is a very welcome adjustment Effendi and it will earn our gratitude for the service you have provided."

At that moment a servant approached and whispered in the clerk's ear. The clerk glanced up and viewed his visitors with a look of added respect, "Our master has requested you join him for lunch. Your companions in the garden are being similarly entertained."

Sinbad, being senior, was the first to respond on their behalf, and thanking the clerk he added,

"We cannot possibly decline the hospitality of such a generous host."

Salem, considering his earlier encounter realised that the invitation could have implications well beyond their expectations. They followed the messenger into a dining room where a table had been prepared with more than ample food for the mid-day meal. There they politely awaited the arrival of their host. An elderly man with a walking stick entered and Salem moved forward to assist him- an offer which was readily accepted. Their host then turned to his servant and informed him that it was a private lunch and that they were not to be disturbed.

"Salem, my son, help me to that white pillow, and seat yourself on my right. Sinbad you can sit directly opposite me, if you will, for I have heard much about you and I wish to view you well". He then added, by way of an introduction, "You may call me 'Old Man' or 'Suleiman Effendi."

"You honour us, Effendi, with such familiarity."

"Sinbad, you must be aware, to a degree, of Salem's extra-ordinary talents. I, myself, have been blessed with such abilities for a considerable time, more years, in fact, than I care to remember."

"Not many complain about the length of tenure granted them by Mother Nature."

"The reason may be that not many are obliged to live as long as I have."

"You have awakened our curiosity, Suleiman Effendi. Surely it cannot be that long."

"You have every right to be inquisitive but I have not discussed this matter with anyone for some centuries".

On hearing this, Sinbad's jaw dropped in disbelief and the sounds he uttered were unintelligible. Salem was not as surprised as his father but was equally enthusiastic to hear Suleiman's story.

"Salem, the information about you and your companion Zahra, was handed down to me by many generations of my kind that preceded me. At one time you must have made a considerable impression on the high-ranking, primordial individuals that you met."

"That was a transient contact. We were later unsure that it actually happened."

"Your encounter indeed took place. It left a lasting impression, of which you must be aware."

"What became of the city we visited? It no longer exists in our present time."

"Many years after your visitation, it was destroyed by an earthquake and the whole region was covered by the sea. The island that you viewed it from reappeared, many millennia later, as a result of another earthquake which separated that land from the mainland. Only a handful of individuals who happened to be working on missions away from the island survived."

"That is very sad to hear and I fear a rather incomplete story for my father but I shall relate the whole tale at a more appropriate time."

"The destruction of the city happened about ninety thousand years ago, and the field officers who survived at the time tried to rescue their families and colleagues but without success."

"Is there any indication of the fate of those humanoids, initially created by the Superior Beings or were they abandoned to their destiny?"

"The only information passed down is more speculative than factual. It is supposed that the small number that survived eventually developed power and capabilities far superior to any possessed by others created later. These extra-ordinary abilities initially alarmed the ordinary humans, or Inferiors, who organised a joint action against the Superiors to further reduce their numbers. This aggressive act of the Inferiors forced the Superiors to use their greater powers to punish them and force them into a subservient state. This led to the concept of God-like beings ruling over mankind."

At that moment, although no door in the room had opened, a fourth person unexpectedly joined them at the table.

"Is there a welcome and an offer of food for a neglected and starving mother-to-be?"

"My dear Lady Zahra, I believe. You are very welcome to my home and anything I have to offer."

Significantly to only Salem's surprise, Zahra reached out and picked a small bunch of whitish-yellow grapes. She considered them carefully and then raised the whole bunch above her head and delicately and seductively lowered it until the lowest grape touched her parted lips.

"My word! No seeds, an excellent aroma and sweet enough to eat! How do they grow them without seeds?"

Salem, still stunned at what he was witnessing managed, "Zahra, my love, do you realise what you have managed to achieve? This is the first time that either of us has, by mental energy, achieved a transfer of our complete body matter in a recognisable form from one location to another."

"It was an instinctive act. I woke up in our bed after an exciting but exhausting visit to the market and found myself alone. I closed my eyes and thought about you, Salem, and there you were in excellent company and enjoying a tray of delicious food. It immediately enticed me to join you."

"I have just looked into our bedroom and it is indeed unoccupied. It is a good thing that the guard outside your door would not dream of disturbing you for other than a dire emergency."

Sinbad, happy to see that all was well calmed Salem, "You are searching for reasons to be concerned, Salem. Let us just appreciate Zahra's presence and enjoy the company of all."

"Father, I am speaking more in amazement than anything else. We have both achieved partial transfer of ourselves from one location to another on numerous occasions. But we have never done this – a complete body transfer involving an effect on solid matter outside our own bodies. This is a completely unexpected achievement on Zahra's part."

"Well, my husband, now we have to accept that this can be accomplished by us."

"My children, you are unique. No-one has ever come close to the level of abilities that you have attained. Even the Atlanteans could not facilitate travel without the use of some form of mechanical assistance. It could well be that your enhanced vibrational state not only enables you to be more receptive than others but allows you to travel through time and matter unimpeded."

"How are you and we related to the Atlanteans, Effendi?"

"A relationship does exist between all humanoids and Atlanteans. We all owe our existence to their initiating efforts. The field technicians that survived decided that there was a good reason for them to continue in existence on this planet. After the catastrophe they spent the many long years of their tenure utilising the knowledge they had accumulated, in the enhancement of their designed project. Later they assisted the project further by allowing their own hereditary factors to become intertwined with those of the local humans. Those transferred factors were stronger and often resulted in beings with extra-ordinary abilities. In the case of you two the blessings seem to be boundless. As a Superior myself I am proud of the way you are handling your phenomenal capabilities."

"Effendi, on the occasion of our visit to the Atlanteans we were informed that they can affect matters within their vision. Could you please explain that?"

"In my understanding that vision had to be a mental one, the one that we call 'the third eye', being far more powerful and more far-reaching than the optical one. For example, Zahra, my dear, when you look at that single grape in your hand, what do you see?"

"I see a perfectly formed mature fruit almost gold in colour and promising a deliciously sweet taste."

"Now look again, using your mind as well as your eyes. Observe the particles that make up the skin and then look through them to the flesh beyond. Salem, you can assist Zahra in her search and report to us what you see."

"We see ever smaller particles moving at speeds impossible to describe. We could not observe these visually or assess their speed. We can observe another universe every time we penetrate a new unit and the most extra-ordinary thing is that some of the particles are separating from the main structure and departing at incredible speed to different destinations."

"Children, return to us now but make your journey slowly for your experience has immensely disturbed your previously expected concepts. The Universe is proving to be infinite in every direction. It may eventually be possible for humans to analyse the immense wealth and intricacy of Nature by enhancing their knowledge of it rather than possessing and consuming it. Only then will it be possible to find a reason for our existence in this fantastic scene and to discover the relevance of humanity within it."

With that, Suleiman placed his hands on their shoulders to aid their gradual return to reality.

Sinbad's understanding of the events he had witnessed was challenged and he turned to Suleiman for enlightenment.

"I am in need of illumination as much as you my friend. My personal contribution to this was only an initial prompting. Salem and Zahra are the only living humans to have such experiences. In the future, humanity may develop to a level where these phenomena might be deemed comprehensible or even common-place."

Salem, then fully recovered, asked, "In what manner can these findings contribute to the knowledge and understanding of our circumstances and could it be possible to explain our extended abilities?"

"My appraisal is instantaneous and therefore lacking in depth. However, first consider the particles you have observed in the grape. I believe that all matter, including our own bodies, is made of such particles. It appears that you have been granted the unique gift of being able to control the movement of these particles. The harmony in your bodies appears at such a level as to provide a relaxed and flexible particle state enabling your powerful spirits to manipulate those particles at will. If the movement of these particles is speeded sufficiently they become energised and your personas become free from the shackles of your physical state. This allows you to pass through time and space. You two, of all people, are able to experience and appreciate the wonders of the natural world in all its many forms."

"Suleiman Effendi, how does that which we have witnessed lead us to an understanding of the concept of life?"

"The understanding of 'life' is relative to the circumstances in which it is being considered. An individual life is normally seen when all the necessary parts of a body are functioning in some level of harmony. This life, as perceived, has a finite span and ceases to exist when that harmony is lost. However, this may also be viewed as one episode in a continuum of life in which many different features, hereditary factors, body matter and spirit energy from the deceased life, become part of a future life and so each life has in some measure a level of infinity. This continuum is in natural balance with the whole of nature. For instance, a grape on a bunch, on the branch of the vine, is a single unit of a life form in harmony with the whole plant as well as depending on its surroundings from the earth to the sky in its need of nutrition and water and energy from the sun. In its turn it provides food for animals and plants and when it dies it continues to provide nutrition for future plants, and life continues. This suggests that it is Mother Nature who holds the balance and ensures the perpetuum of life. Ancient peoples have always been aware of this in their worship of Nature. The Turku people revered Tanri, their goddess of earth and fertility, whom they believed brought their crops seasonally to sustain them. Eventually her name became synonymous with all nature. The fields, mountains, seas, earth, and sky all became one."

"Effendi, all this has neglected the concept of Sheitan. Where does evil feature in our everyday lives?"

"It is possible that your father, with his vast experience of the lives of men, has a better understanding of this than most. Sinbad, to what do you attribute the origin of evil, as its influence seems to be ever-present in human affairs?"

"Sheitan, in my opinion is the personification of choices made by individuals. It is the antithesis of goodness. At every turn life provides us with choices which invariably have opposite results, one may promote the good and well-being of others with perhaps, little benefit to ourselves, while the alternative is heavily weighted by self-interest. The continual choice of self-interest and the increasing disregard for the good of others eventually leads to the deterioration of human values and only evil can result."

"Effendi, it is obvious that the teaching of the world's religions have a part to play in man's choices. Where does Islam stand in relation to the other religions in this regard?"

"Children, I was a member of the welcoming group of City Elders when Mohammed walked through the city gates of Jerusalem for the first time. True to his principles of equality, the master was on foot while his manservant took his turn on their camel.

From that day to this I have recognised Mohammed as the greatest proponent of a Rule of Law for Mankind. That is not to say that other religions are wrong and I am of the belief that many have much common ground in their teaching. However, it is Islam with which I am most familiar. Unfortunately, however noble the principles, it is possible for mankind to misinterpret and corrupt the teaching for their own ends. One of the greatest values of the Sunni sect of Islam is its flexibility. It is meant to be advisory and must be related to time and circumstances."

When Sinbad, on behalf of them all, asked how they could ever be of service to the Old Gentleman he was told, "The service that Salem and Zahra have already contributed to humanity is great. They have healed the sick and used their powers to minimise the effects of combat in various conflict situations. They are well-known in powerful circles and I was deemed suitable to follow their activities, to report back to Higher Authority and to offer assistance to them when necessary."

This last remark sparked Salem's curiosity and he interrupted, "You said you were watching for us- how was our presence brought to your attention?"

"The teacher who offered your first instruction alerted me to your presence and your ways."

This consoled Salem as he knew Musa to be always concerned for him and to be watching over him from afar.

Suleiman continued, "For the past hundred years or so I have been participating in the organisation of cross-border trading. I have also acted as a medium for the enlightened and arranged many psychic contacts and communications. The presence of you two was initially brought to my attention by this communication network. This network has also been used to promote trade and this has been instrumental with my amassing a large fortune which is of no value to me except as a means to facilitate.

I have been feeling very old for a long time and now

that we have met I believe that it is time for me to hand all this over for your care and to release my hold on life."

"How sure are you of the choice you are making?"

"I had decided this some time ago, when I first heard of your ability. I see that you have used the exceptional gifts that nature has bestowed on you to the full and for the benefit of others. Society needs many more like you. When you look at your own reflection in the water you see your true self; there is no false image and I know that you will always be true to yourself and that is good enough for me. I have been merely waiting to meet you to share my decision. After the twins are born, at a time of your choosing, you will return here and find everything in order awaiting you. All personnel here are well-versed in their tasks and will serve you loyally as they have served me.

One thing I must advise you- to observe total secrecy of your abilities even from your mother. Her maternal pride could lead her to an indiscretion that could harm you. I have found that most people tend to be prejudiced against the unknown and the unexplained, and this may lead them to take dangerous action."

At this the Old Gentleman wished them God's Speed and the travellers took their leave.

Zahra discreetly returned to her room in the same manner that she had left it. Gathering the rest of the party from the courtyard, Sinbad and Salem took the road to the caravanserai to join her. Salem carefully carried a small casket, heavy with gold and the documents of information on his new role.

TWENTY-TWO

LIFE GOES ON

Forty remarkable memorable days had passed since their arrival in Basra and Bathsheba was still beside herself with unlimited joy. She would walk around the palace with tears in her eyes almost unable to believe that she was so blessed.

Even on their arrival she had been delighted to notice that Salem was wearing the short-sleeved jacket she had so lovingly made him for his journey. When she drew attention to this, Salem explained to all around that the jacket was his lucky charm as not only was it given him with his mother's love but it had actually prevented a serious injury when a crossbow bolt had struck him a glancing blow. Hearing this, Sinbad examined the jacket more carefully to discover the cause of this special protection and then enlightened everyone present by explaining that the fabric was woven not from silk, as it appeared, but from the silk-like threads from the web of a rare spider from Madagascar. The threads were lighter and stronger than any steel he had ever seen.

The day was hot and Salem and Zahra had retired to their room after lunch to rest, as was the custom. Zahra was becoming very frustrated by the restrictions being forced on her by her well-meaning but over-protective mother-in-law. She was sitting up high in the bed leaning against a large pile of cushions. From there she could watch a small number of sailing boats, pretty with their tall sails extended to maximise the light noon breeze, as they glided across the conflux of the two rivers, the Euphrates and the Tigris. The boatmen were having to assist the sails but were pulling on the oars half-heartedly in the heat. Everything appeared to be drifting. There seemed no need for hurry in this idyllic tableau of waterways and lakes.

Salem sat down on the bed next to Zahra and took both her hand reassuringly to ease her tension. An understanding smile spread across her face and her eyes brightened as she asked, "Salem, tell me about your grandfather."

"In real life I have never met him."

"Shall we go and visit him now? I am sure he will welcome it as a pleasant surprise. No-one here will know as we are never disturbed in our room and we will not be expected until dinner and will be back by then."

"May be we can follow the journey that I took before."

"That would be perfect. Come lie next to me and hold my hand. I know you have been worried lately about the control of your wealth but your grandfather is just the person to give you advice."

Salem joined her on the large bed without even removing his slippers. They closed their eyes and focussed on the terrain around them as they drifted from Basra down the Tigris River which carelessly abandoned its water to the reeds and marshes that cluttered the silted shoreline, before finally enriching the waters of the Persian Gulf. From here they followed the water through the Straits of Hormuz and into the Indian Ocean. The Oman coastline led on to Hadhramauti and soon Aden was beneath them. Here Salem remembered the nightmare he had suffered when cavalry archers and spearmen, seated on big black birds, had attacked him over Aden harbour. At this they both laughed. At Aden they turned south, this time without having to consider wind or tidal direction. However, the clear air did allow excellent views throughout their journey. First Mogadishu, then Mombasa were passed and then the city of Zanzibar was the last harbour before they turned east over the ocean to their destination, Vohemar, in the north-east of the very large island of Madagascar. As they travelled they took note of the variety of life-styles that were imposed on people by the differing natural resources. They were delighted and impressed by the animal and birdlife they encountered on their way.

As they neared their destination they could see two elderly gentlemen, comfortably seated on cushions placed on a large colourful carpet amongst the flowerbeds in a secluded courtyard garden. Salem recognised both the gentlemen and indicated to Zahra to materialise gently. The old men, although delighted, did not seem surprised and Salem was sure they had prior knowledge of their visitors.

Musa, for it was he who was Masood's guest, greeted his former student with great affection and Masood, himself, was overjoyed.

Salem, closely followed by Zahra, approached the two men and, going down on one knee in front of each in turn, took the proffered hand and kissing it lifted it to their foreheads in a sign of deep respect.

Musa was the first to speak, "Salam aleykum, Salem, it is a wonderful and unexpected pleasure to see you again. Do be so kind to introduce your stunning companion."

His grandfather followed with "Salem, my grandson, thanks to Allah that finally I have been able to lay eyes on you. Now introduce your beautiful and very welcome companion then sit and take some refreshment with us."

"We thank you for many things grandfather and also you, my much valued teacher. We shall take refreshment with you and this wonderful lady is my wife, Zahra, who insisted on this journey, so eager was she to meet you."

Salem then proceeded to explain the reason for their journey and tried briefly to give an account of some of the past events, including the means they used to accomplish their visit.

The evening drew near and they fell quiet as they listened to a pair of nightingales practising their courtship rituals. Their song had been lingering in the background for a time when it reached a crescendo of perfect harmony breaking the transient silence.

Zahra, moved to tears at the sound, turned away to hide her emotion. It was then she noticed a small kitten readying to pounce upon the sweethearts. She screamed in anticipation of the horror to come.

The hunt was on before anyone could react. Salem tried to deflect the kitten's spring away from its intended prey but the momentum only succeeded in carrying it within striking distance of the bird, where it reached out a paw and made contact with it.

The attack ended the song of one and turned the other into a wild screech. Salem moved fast enough to catch the bird in his open palm before it fell to the ground under the cat's blow, and immediately started his process of life preservation. He feared the futility of his efforts but did not cease his attempt.

Zahra, overcoming her initial shock and despair, cupped her hands over Salem's to reinforce his power.

The two elders sat silent and motionless.

Tears from Zahra's eyes were now flowing freely. She was witnessing the gradual deterioration of the tiny creature's inner harmony and realised that Salem's efforts may not be sufficient to halt the inevitable. Pearls of her tears trickled through her shaking fingers and the droplets touched the dying bird just as its spirit was on the point of taking its leave.

Suddenly Zahra's tears turned to a smile. The powerful empathy of her tears had held the departing spirit and had flowed through the small frame restoring its vital harmony.

A stirring in the animal beneath her hand was sensed by the other bird, who felt the upsurge of life and joined in the celebration with a soaring cadenza of joyous song.

Musa turned to his old friend, suffused with an immense pride exclaimed, "They helped her back to life! It is a miracle!"

Salem and Zahra held hands as they watched the two love birds on the branch and silently wondered if perhaps, this time they may have overstepped their boundaries.

NEVER AN END ALWAYS A BEGINNING

AUTHOR'S NOTE

In an attempt to stay as true as possible to the stories told by my aunt, I have been obliged to take certain liberties with history.

While King Philip Augustus of France was certainly in the places mentioned at that time, he would not have had a wife with him. His first wife Isabel had died the previous year in child-birth and he did not re-marry until two years later when he married Ingeborg of Denmark in 1193.

Although Isaac Comnenus had a base in Limassol, the actual castle was not built until two years later when Guy de Lusignan started construction in 1193.

Comnenus's remarks about the possibility of wooing Berengaria were almost certainly fictitious as he had a wife, an Armenian princess and also a daughter, known as the Damsel of Cyprus, both residing in Kyrenia Castle.

According to history Comnenus was not abandoned at sea but incarcerated at Apostolos Andreas on the Karpaz peninsular where he was reputed to have been held by Richard, not in irons, but in silver chains. He was later taken to Lebanon in the custody of the Knights Hospitallers and finally to Austria where he died of poisoning in 1195.

I crave my readers' pardon for these licences.